Coyote Tales

Of The
Native American Indians

Written and Edited by G.W. Mullins
With Original Art by C.L. Hause

ISBN: 978-1-7377100-6-6

First Edition Printing

Light Of The Moon Publishing has allowed this work to remain exactly as the author intended, verbatim, without editorial input.

Printed in the United States of America

The following book represents a collection of Native American works which are public domain. You may have read the stories before. In true story telling fashion, the stories have been left as close to the original form as possible. In Native American culture, in order to pass the stories along with all information intact, they had to be told pretty much word for word, to keep the legends alive. Many of these stories were translated directly from original Native language texts. With that in mind, please be aware that some spellings and word usage may vary from one tribe to another. For instance, the spelling of "teepee", as used in this book, can also be written as "tipi", and "tepee". All are correct. Also, when using words like "someone", in most native cultures, it would be "some one". So, keep in mind, these are not necessarily misspellings. They are simply dialect and translations.

This book is dedicated to Vince Mullins, my Grandfather (Pawpaw). He was a tall red man with fire in his eyes… who I loved so much.

This book is also dedicated to one of my heroes Chief Dan George, a true visionary.

G.W. Mullins

Chief Dan George, (July 24, 1899 – September 23, 1981) was a chief of the Tsleil-Waututh Nation, a Coast Salish band located on Burrard Inlet in North Vancouver, British Columbia, Canada. He was also an author, poet, actor, and an Officer of the Order of Canada. At the age of 71, he was nominated for an Academy Award for Best Supporting Actor in Little Big Man.

You have noticed that everything as Indian does is in a circle, and that is because the Power of the World always works in circles, and everything tries to be round.... The Sky is round, and I have heard that the earth is round like a ball, and so are all the stars. The wind, in its greatest power, whirls. Birds make their nest in circles, for theirs is the same religion as ours....
~Black Elk, Oglala Sioux Holy Man, 1863-1950

Coyote Tales Of The Native American Indians

Also Available From G.W. Mullins And C.L. Hause

War Song Tales Of The Native American Indians

Walking With Spirits Native American Myths, Legends, And Folklore
Volumes One Thru Six

The Native American Cookbook

Native American Cooking - An Indian Cookbook With Legends And Folklore

The Native American Story Book - Stories Of The American Indians For Children
Volumes One Thru Five

The Best Native American Stories For Children

Cherokee A Collection of American Indian Legends, Stories And Fables

Creation Myths - Tales Of The Native American Indians

Strange Tales Of The Native American Indians

Spirit Quest - Stories Of The Native American Indians

Animal Tales Of The Native American Indians

Medicine Man - Shamanism, Natural Healing, Remedies And Stories Of The Native
American Indians

Native American Legends: Stories Of The Hopi Indians
Volumes One and Two

Totem Animals Of The Native Americans

The Best Native American Myths, Legends And Folklore
Volumes One Thru Three

Ghosts, Spirits And The Afterlife In Native American Indian Mythology And
Folklore

The Native American Art Book – Art Inspired By Native American Myths And
Legends

Star People, Sky Gods And Other Tales Of The Native American Indians

Animal Tales Of The native American Indians Vol. 2

Origin Tales Of The Native American Indians

THE NATIVE AMERICAN
STORY COLLECTION SERIES
Featuring The Writing Of Best-Selling Author
G.W. MULLINS
And Original Art From
Award Winning Artist C.L. HAUSE

This is the Earth, healed again, growing green and blue.
I want you to remember this exactly as it is,
and then go and tell the people that if enough of us hold this
image in their minds,
we can heal the Earth and make it like it was a long time ago.
- Grandfather Rolling Thunder, Cherokee Medicine Elder

Lakota Instructions for Living

Friend do it this way - that is,
whatever you do in life,
do the very best you can
with both your heart and mind.

And if you do it that way,
the Power Of The Universe
will come to your assistance,
if your heart and mind are in Unity.

When one sits in the Hoop Of The People,
one must be responsible because
All of Creation is related.
And the hurt of one is the hurt of all.
And the honor of one is the honor of all.
And whatever we do affects everything in the
universe.

If you do it that way - that is,
if you truly join your heart and mind
as One - whatever you ask for,
that's the Way It's Going To Be.

Passed down from White Buffalo Calf Woman

Table of Contents

Introduction

Native American Mythology began long before the European settlers arrived on North American soil. Contrary to popular beliefs, there is more to Native American Folklore than stories of buffalo hunts, teepee living and animal stories. Hundreds of tribes throughout North American created a huge mythological system that has rivaled that of the Greeks. Many of these tales have been lost, or are often hard to find. This collection represents a history that should be remembered.

As a Native American myself, I embrace these stories. Native Americans tribes offer such a rich heritage. They have recorded a huge amount of their history through storytelling. In these stories you will relive their history and the lives of North America's First People.

The stories in this book have been handed down from generation to generation. And in such tradition, they are now handed down to you, to share with the next generation.

Included in this anthology, are a group of collected works from the well-known, to the often-forgotten tribes. The tales included within this book feature one of the most familiar animals in Native American folklore, the trickster known as the Coyote. Often deceptive and always out for himself, the Coyote was often the bad guy in stories, as you will read in the folklore within this collection.

The Great Spirit Names the Animal People: How Coyote Came by His Powers

(Okanogan)
from Mourning Dove (Hum-isha-ma;
Christal Quintasket), Coyote Tales
(1933)

The Great Spirit called all his people together from all over the earth. There was to be a change. He would give names to the people, and the Animal World was to rule. The naming was to begin at the break of day, each one having the right to choose his or her name according to who came first to the Spirit Chief's lodge. The Spirit Chief would also give each one their duty to perform in the changed conditions.

It was the night before the New World. Excitement was among the people. Each one desired a great name of note. All wished to be awake and first at the lodge of the Great Spirit Chief. Everyone wanted power to rule some tribe, some kingdom of the Animal World.

Coyote was of a degraded nature, a vulgar type of life. He was an imitator of everything that he saw or heard. When he asked a question, when he asked for information and it was given him, he would always say, "I knew that before! I did not have to be told." That was Coyote's way. He was hated by all the people for his ways. No one liked him. He boasted too much about his wisdom, about everything.

Coyote went among the anxious people, bragging to everyone how early he was going to rise, how he would be the first one at the Spirit Chief's lodge. He bragged of the great name he would choose. He said, "I will have three big names to select from: there is Grizzly Bear, who will be ruler over all running, four-footed animals; Eagle, who will lead all the flying birds; Salmon, who will be chief over all the fish of every kind."

Coyote's twin brother, who took the name of Fox, said to him, "Do not be too sure. Maybe no one will be given his choice of names. Maybe you will have to retain your own name, Coyote. Because it is a degraded name, no one among the tribes will want to take it.

. . . .

Coyote went to his tepee in anger. He determined not to sleep that night. He would remain awake so as to be the first at the Spirit Chief's lodge for the name he wanted. . . . Coyote's wife (afterwards Mole), sat on her feet at the side of the doorway. She looked up at Coyote and said in a disappointed tone, "Have you no food for the children? They are starving! I can find no roots to dig."

"Eh-ha!" grunted Coyote sarcastically. He answered his wife, "I am no common person to be spoken to in that fashion by a mere woman. Do you know that I am going to be a great Chief at daybreak tomorrow? I shall be Grizzly Bear. I will devour my enemies with ease. I will take other men's wives. I will need you no longer. You are growing too old, too ugly to be the wife of a great warrior, of a big Chief as I will be."

. . . .

Coyote ordered his wife to gather plenty of wood for the tepee fire where he would sit without sleep all night. Half of the night passed; Coyote grew sleepy. His eyes would close however hard he tried to keep them open. Then he thought what to do. He took two small sticks and braced his eyelids apart. He must not sleep! But before Coyote knew it, he was fast asleep. He was awakened by his wife, Mole, when she returned from the Spirit Chief's lodge, when the sun was high in the morning sky.

Coyote jumped up from where he lay. He hurried to the lodge of the Chief Spirit. Nobody was there, and Coyote thought that he was first. He went into the lodge and spoke, "I am going to be Grizzly Bear!"

The Chief answered, "Grizzly Bear was taken at daybreak!"

Coyote said, "Then I shall be called Eagle!"

The Chief answered Coyote, "Eagle has chosen his name. He flew away long ago."

Coyote then said, "I think that I will be called Salmon."

The Spirit Chief Informed Coyote, "Salmon has also been taken. All the names have been used except your own: Coyote. No one wished to steal your name from you."

Poor Coyote's knees grew weak. He sank down by the fire in that great tepee. The heart of the Spirit Chief was touched when he saw the lowered head of Coyote, the mischief-maker. After a silence the Chief spoke, "You are Coyote! You are the hated among all the tribes, among all the people. I have chosen you from among all others to make you sleep, to go to the land of the dream visions. I make a purpose for you, a big work for you to do before another change comes to the people. You are to be father for all the tribes, for all the new kind of people who are to come. Because you are so hated, degraded and despised, you will be known as the Trick-person. You will have power to change yourself into anything, any object you wish when in danger or distress. There are man-eating monsters on the earth who are destroying the people. The tribes cannot increase and grow as I wish. These monsters must all be vanquished before the new people come. This is your work to do. I give you powers to kill these monsters. I have given your twin brother, Fox, power to help you, to restore you to life should you be killed. Your bones may be scattered; but if there is one hair left on your body, Fox can bring you back to life. Now go, despised Coyote! Begin the work laid out for your trail. Do good for the benefit of your people."

Thus, Coyote of the Animal People was sent about the earth to fight and destroy the people-devouring monsters, to prepare the land for the coming of the new people, the Indians. Coyote' eyes grew slant from the effects of the sticks with which he braced them open that night when waiting for the dawn of the name giving day. From this, the Indians have inherited their slightly slant eyes as descendants from Coyote.

Tale of Coyote and the Origin of Death

(Caddo)
Dorsey, George A.
Traditions of the
Caddo. Washington:
Carnegie Institution.
1905.

In the beginning of this
world there was no
such thing as death.
Every one continued to
live until there were so
many people that there was not room for any more on the
earth. The chiefs held a council to determine what to do.
One man arose and said that he thought it would be a good
plan to have the people die and be gone for a little while,
and then to return. As soon as he sat down Coyote jumped
up and said that he thought that people ought to die forever,
for this little world was not large enough to hold all of the
people, and if the people who died came back to life there
would not be food enough for all. All of the other men
objected, saying that they did not want their friends and
relatives to die and be gone forever, for then people would
grieve and worry and there would not be any happiness in
the world.

All except Coyote decided to have the people die and be
gone for a little while, and then to come back to life.

The medicine-men built a large grass house facing the east,
and when they had completed it, they called all of the men
of the tribe together and told them that they had decided to
have the people who died come to the medicine-house and

there be restored to life. The chief medicine-man said that he would put a large white and black eagle feather on top of the grass house, and that when the feather became bloody and fell over, the people would know that some one had died. Then all of the medicine-men were to come to the grass house and sing. They would sing a song that would call the spirit of the dead to the grass house, and when the spirit came, they would cause it to assume the form that it had while living, and then they would restore it to life again. All of the people were glad when the medicine men announced these rules about death, for they were anxious for the dead to be restored to life and come again to live with them.

After a time, they saw the eagle feather turn bloody and fall, and so they knew that some one had died. The medicine-men assembled in the grass house and sang, as they had promised that they would, for the spirit of the dead to come to them. In about ten days a whirlwind blew from the west, circled about the grass house, and finally, entered through the entrance in the east. From the whirlwind appeared a handsome young man who had been murdered by another tribe. All of the people saw him and rejoiced except Coyote, who was displeased because his rules about dead were not carried out. In a short time, the feather became bloody and fell again. Coyote saw it and at once went to the grass house. He took his seat near the door, and there sat with the singers for many days, and when at last he heard the whirlwind coming he slipped near the door, and as the whirlwind circled about the house and was about to enter, he closed the door. The spirit in the whirlwind, finding the door closed, whirled on by. Death forever was then introduced, and people from that time on grieved about the dead and were unhappy. Now whenever any one meets a whirlwind or hears the wind whistle, he says: "There is some one wandering about." Ever since Coyote closed the door the spirits of the dead have wandered over the earth, trying to find some place to go, until at last they find the road to spirit land.

Coyote jumped up and ran away and never came back, for when he saw what he had done he was afraid. Ever after that he ran from one place to another, always looking back over first one shoulder and then over the other, to see if any one was pursuing him, and ever since then he has been starving, for no one will give him anything to eat.

Creation Myth
(Nez Perce)

Once Porcupine was going along the river bank looking for food. Soon he saw some fine, fat buffalo, ten of them, just across the river. Then Porcupine wanted to get across the river, but could not. After some thought he called to the buffalo to stand in line. This was so that he could tell which one was the fattest. Then he picked out the fattest one and told him to swim across the river. When this buffalo came up to Porcupine, he asked Porcupine where he wanted to sit, on his back or on his tail. Porcupine answered, "I would rather be under your forelegs, so I shall not drown."

The buffalo agreed. When they were nearly across, Porcupine struck the buffalo under the foreleg with a large knife. So, he killed that buffalo, but the others ran away.

Porcupine was looking for something with which to sharpen his knife. He was singing, "I wish I could find something with which to sharpen my knife, for I haven't had any fat buffalo yet." Now, Coyote happened to be going by and he heard Porcupine singing. Coyote came up to him and Porcupine was afraid. Coyote asked him what he was singing, and Porcupine answered, "I was not singing anything, I was just saying I wish I had some string for my moccasin." Coyote said, "No, you did not say that; I heard what you said." Porcupine said nothing more; so, Coyote told him what he had killed. Coyote said, "Now, I have a sharp knife, so I can help you." Then Coyote said, "Let us try jumping over the buffalo; the one who jumps over may have it all. I'll try first." Coyote succeeded, but Porcupine did not, so Coyote got all the meat. Then Coyote took his sharp knife and cut Porcupine's head, but did not kill him.

Now, Coyote had some children: one of them was with him, and the rest were at home. Coyote said to his child, "I am going after the other children. You watch the old Porcupine, and if he gets up you call me and I will come back and kill him." When Coyote was gone, Porcupine got up. The young Coyote cried, "Father, Porcupine is up." Then Coyote hurried back and asked his baby what the matter was. The child said, "He was trying to take some of the buffalo meat, but now he is quiet again." Coyote started off a second time.

When he was a great way off Porcupine got up. The child called his father, but this time in vain. Porcupine struck the young Coyote with a stone and killed him. Then he set the child up under a tree and stuffed his mouth full of buffalo fat. Then Porcupine took all the meat to the top of a tree and watched for Coyote and his family to come.

When Coyote with his wife and children had come up close, Coyote said to the children, "Look at your brother; he is eating and having a great time." But when they arrived, they saw that the baby was killed and had his mouth stuffed with fat. Then Coyote was very angry. He wondered where Porcupine had gone. When Coyote looked up, he saw Porcupine sitting in a tall tree laughing. Coyote said, "Please come down"; but Porcupine answered, "I do not like you because you are trying to cheat me out of my buffalo meat." Coyote said, "Just give us a little piece of fat or meat." Then Porcupine told Coyote and his family to all stand together under the tree. They did this. Then Porcupine dropped the buffalo head down on them and they were all killed.

How the Old Man Made People

Long ago, when the world was new, there was no one living in it at all, except the Old Man,

Na-pe, and his sometimes-friend and sometimes-enemy A-pe'si, the Coyote, and a few buffalo. There were no other people and no other animals. But the Old Man changed all that. He changed it first because he was lonely, and then because he was lazy; and maybe be shouldn't have, but anyway, he did. And this was the way of it.

Na-pe was sitting by his fire one day, trying to think of some way to amuse himself. He had plenty to eat--a whole young buffalo; no need to go hunting. He had a lodge; no work to do; and a fire. He was comfortable, but he wasn't contented. His only companion, A-pe'si the Coyote, was off somewhere on some scheme of his own, and anyway he had quarreled with A-pe'si, and they were on bad terms; so even if he had been there, Old Man would still have been lonely. He poked some sticks in the fire, threw a rock or two in the river, lit his pipe, and walked around. . . then sat down, and thought how nice it would be to have someone to smoke with, and to talk to. "Another one, like me," he thought. And he poked some more sticks in the fire, and threw some more rocks in the river.

Then he thought, "Why not? I am the Old Man! I can make anything I want to. Why shouldn't I make another like me, and have a companion?" And he promptly went to work. First, he found a little still pool of water, and looked at his reflection carefully, so as to know just what he wanted to make. Then he counted his bones as best he could, and felt the shape of them.

Next, he went and got some clay, modelled a lot of bones, and baked them in his fire. When they were all baked, he took them out and looked at them. Some of them were very good, but others were crooked, or too thin, or had broken in the baking. These he put aside in a little heap.

Then he began to assemble the best of the clay bones into a figure of a man. He tied them all together with buffalo sinews, and smoothed them all carefully with buffalo fat. He padded them with clay mixed with buffalo blood, and stretched over the whole thing skin taken from the inside of the buffalo. Then he sat down and lit his pipe again.

He looked at the man he had made rather critically. It wasn't exactly what he had wanted, but still it was better than nothing.

"I will make some more," said Na-pe.

He picked the new man up and blew smoke into his eyes, nose, and mouth, and the figure came to life. Na-pe sat him down by the fire, and handed him the pipe. Then he went to get more clay.

All day long Na-pe worked, making men. It took a long time, because some of the bones in each lot weren't good, and he must discard them and make others. But at last, he got several men, all sitting by the fire and passing the pipe around. Na-pe sat down with them, and was very happy. He left the heap of discarded bones where they were, at the doorway of his lodge.

So, Na-pe and the men lived in his camp, and the men learned to hunt, and Na-pe had company, someone to smoke with, and they were all quite contented.

But the heap of left-over bones was a nuisance. Every time one of the men went in or out of Na-pe's lodge, they tripped over the bones. The wind blew through them at night, making a dreadful noise. The bones frequently tumbled over, making more of a disturbance. Na-pe intended to throw them in the river, but he was a bit lazy, and never got around to it. So, the left-over bones stayed where they were.

By this time A-pe'si, the Coyote, was back from wherever he had been. He went around the camp, looking the men over, and being very superior, saying that he didn't think much of Na-pe's handiwork. He was also critical of the heap of bones at the door of the lodge. "I should think you would do something with them--make them into men," said A-pe'si, the Coyote.

"All right, I will," said Na-pe. "Only they aren't very good. It will be difficult to make men out of them!" "Oh, I'll help, I'll help!" said A-pe'si. "With my cleverness, we will make something much better than these poor creatures of yours!"

So, the two of them set to work. The discarded bones, clicking and tattling, were sorted out, and tied together.

Then Na-pe mixed the clay and the buffalo blood to cover them. He fully intended to make the bones into men, but A-pe'si the Coyote kept interfering; consequently, when the job was done, the finished product was quite different. Na-pe surveyed it dubiously, but he blew the smoke into its eyes and nose and mouth, as he had with the men. And the woman came to life.

A-pe'si and Na-pe made the rest of the bones into women, and as they finished each one, they put them all together, and the women immediately began to talk to each other. A-pe'si was very pleased with what he had done. "When I made my men," said Na-pe, "I set them down by the fire to smoke."

And even to this day, if you have one group of men, and another of women, the men will want to sit by the fire and smoke. But the women talk. And whether it is because they were made out of the left-over bones that clicked and rattled, or whether it is because A-pe'si, the Coyote --who is a noisy creature himself--had a part in their making, no one can say.

Coyote Frees the Buffalo

Coyote and his family were living for a long time in a village near the plains that were his hunting grounds. The hunting was good, for there were many buffalo, but one summer, there were none. Coyote and the other hunters traveled for many miles and found not one. Everyone in the village grew thin with hunger. Coyote's children cried because their bellies were empty.

"The buffalo are somewhere," Coyote said to himself. So, the next morning, and the morning after that, and the morning after that, he went out looking. "Somewhere I shall find the buffalo," he told himself each morning. "Why is it that I cannot?"

One day he did not go out onto the planes, but into the woods. Deep in the woods he climbed to the top of a knoll.

A wind was blowing there, and in the wind, Coyote smelled meat. He stood still and sniffed again. Yes, meat! Buffalo meat! Coyote lifted his nose and followed the smell. He followed it for miles, up and down, across creeks, and through brambles and brush. This smell grew stronger and stronger until he came at last to a lodge that stood by itself at the edge of a wood. Beyond the wood a high bluff rose above the trees.

Coyote's nose told him that the meat was nearby, but it told him, too, that this was a bad place, so he hid in the bushes and watched. Soon he saw a small child come out of the lodge to play. The child ran all around the lodge. He threw stones at a tree. At last, he went to sit in the doorway of the lodge and deep in the earth with a stick.

Coyote grinned, and turned himself into a small, fat puppy. His coat was brown and black and silky. His eyes and nose were soft. But he forgot to change his whiskers and his eyes. He gave a little yipping bark, and tumbled out of his hiding place.

The little boy looked up and saw him. "Puppy!" he cried. "Puppy come!" And he ran toward Coyote-Pup and took him in his arms. "Father!" he cried as he ran into the lodge. "Father, look! I found a puppy!"

Crow, who was his father, looked at Coyote-Pup and frowned. "That is not a pup. Something is different about it. Something wrong."

"No! It is a puppy!" The child held Coyote-Pup closer.

"No, it is something different, not a real pup," Crow said. "It will be dark soon. Take it out and put it where you found it."

"I will not! It is my puppy. I want to keep it!"

His father frowned. "You cannot. Take it out."

"I won't!"

"Hoh! You will not? Well then, bring it here. We will see whether it is a pup or not," Crow said. He held Coyote-Pup out toward the cook fire and, as it came close to the flames, the pup gave a yip, and wriggled, and made water into the fire.

"Ha!" Crow laughed. "It is a pup! Take him and give him some meat to eat."

So, the child did, and Coyote-Pup ate it all up and begged for more. Later, after dark, when the fire had burned down to coals, Crowe and his son went to their beds, and Coyote-Pup curled up beside the fire. The others soon fell asleep, but Coyote listened, and only pretended to sleep. When it was safe, he turned back into his own shape, slipped out the door, and followed his nose into the night.

His nose led him through the moonlight to the bluff behind the trees behind the lodge. The bluff looked like solid rock, but Coyote's nose told him that there was an opening. He sniffed and sniffed until he came to a crack. He followed the crack. A door. There was a door. He pushed, but it was closed fast. He could find no handle to pull. "Poh!" he said. "Open yourself!"

And the door opened itself.

"Ee-ow!" Coyote yelped and jumped out of the way just in time. A big bull buffalo charged out through the door, and after him thundered cows and bulls and calves, herds of them, and often buffalo to people all of the plains. Coyote danced up and down and urged, "Go, go, go!" as they passed. When the last of the buffalo had run out, Coyote pushed the door shut and hurried after them as they spread out and away toward the plains.

Inside the lodge, Crow woke and heard the thunder of hooves. "Buffalo going by," he thought sleepily. "It is good that all miners shut up." But he was uneasy, and he rose to go out and make sure. When he came to the rocky bluff, he opened the rock door, saw that the caverns were empty, and shouted out to his son, "They are all gone! I knew that pup was no pup!"

When coyote reached his own village, he called out, "Hoh, everyone! I, Coyote, have brought buffalo for our hunters to hunt. Take up your bows and arrows, and go after them!"

Tale of Coyote Becomes a Buffalo

*(Caddo)
Dorsey, George A. Traditions of the Caddo.
Washington: Carnegie Institution. 1905.*

While Coyote was out hunting something to eat, he met Buffalo, who was very powerful among his tribe. He was eating grass and looked fat and well fed. Coyote asked him if he would give him power to turn into a Buffalo and eat grass as he did.

Buffalo said: "Yes, I will give you the power which was given to me by the Great-Father-Above, but when I give you the power you must not use it every chance you get, but only when very necessary." He told Coyote to stand facing the other way and not to move, but to be brave as he was.

Coyote stood still, wondering what was going to happen to him. Buffalo began to throw up dirt with his hoofs and to act very angrily. He told Coyote to keep his eyes closed. Then he made a plunge toward him, and when he was about to strike him with his horns, Coyote jumped out of the way, and Buffalo passed him without touching him. He did this the second, third, fourth, fifth, and sixth times, but the seventh time he stood there without moving. He could hear Buffalo coming at him, but he stood there awaiting what would happen to him. Buffalo struck him and rolled him under his stomach with his horns and threw him up into the air. When he came down on his feet he was turned into a very young Buffalo.

He began to eat green grass at once. Then the old Buffalo told him that if he wanted to turn into a Coyote again, he must find a Buffalo wallow, roll himself over two or three times, and then he would arise a Coyote. Again, Buffalo cautioned him not to use his power too often, telling him that the power was good for only seven times, and he also told him that he must not give the power to any one else, especially to any of his own race.

Before they parted the real Buffalo told Coyote to change back into a Coyote, and he did so, and then they both went on their way. Before Coyote had gone far from Buffalo, he wanted to try his power to see if he could use it alone. He did, and became a Buffalo. During that same day he tried his power three or four times, and before he had met any one he had tried it six times, and had turned himself into a Buffalo for the seventh time.

While he was a Buffalo, he met one of his own people, a famous Coyote, and so he went up to him and said: "Do not you want me to give you some of my power, so that you can eat grass as I do? You look as though you were very hungry." "Yes," said Coyote. "Well, all right," said Coyote-Buffalo. "Go off a short distance from me and stand there and face the other way. Do not run, but be brave as I am. Close your eyes. Now, I am ready," and so he started at him, but the other Coyote jumped out of the way every time until the last time came. Then Coyote stood his ground, and Coyote-Buffalo rolled him under his stomach, and they both went up in the air and came down on their feet. They were both Coyotes, and they stood looking at each other for a time; then they separated and went off.

Tale of Coyote, the Deer, and the Wind

(Caddo)
Dorsey, George A.
Traditions of the Caddo.
Washington: Carnegie
Institution. 1905.

One time when Coyote was out hunting something to eat, he met Deer. Deer asked Coyote where he was going, and Coyote told him that he was going out hunting. Deer asked Coyote how he killed his game, for he noticed that he carried no bow and arrows. "I can kill anything I can get my hands on," said Coyote. "But how do you get close enough to get your hands on your game?" Deer asked. "Sometimes I run the game down, sometimes I catch them asleep." Deer said: "I am considered good food; even the human beings are very fond of my flesh. If you can catch me, I will let you kill me and eat me."

Deer started to run, and Coyote started after him, but soon lost sight of him and gave out. He went on home, but he could not help thinking of Deer's offer, and wondering how he could catch him. He wandered about trying to find him asleep, but never did.

One time, after Coyote had been out searching to find Deer asleep, he grew very tired and lay down in the tall grass to take a nap. When he awoke he heard some one singing near by. He was badly frightened and sat up straight and rubbed his eyes and peeped about. He saw no one, but as he sat still and listened again, he heard his name mentioned in the song. He jumped up and ran as fast as he could; yet he always heard the voice singing in his ears, just as near as when he woke up. He ran as fast and far as he could; then he dropped down to die.

While he was panting, he heard the voice again, and it was so near that he heard these words: "If Coyote ever kills a Deer he shall be as fleet as he, and I who am singing am going to give him power to catch a Deer. I am the Wind." Coyote's fear vanished, and he arose and barked at the Wind in a loud voice, to give thanks. His weariness left him and he started out to find Deer.

He traveled all day, but could not find him. At night he came to a camp, where he stole a buffalo robe. He put the robe over him and then went on to look for Deer. Down by the river he thought he saw him. He went another way and slipped round a bend in the river until he came close to Deer. He reached out his hands to grab him and said, as he caught hold of him: "I have you; I thought you said I could not get you." To his surprise he found that he did not have Deer, but the man whose robe he had stolen.

The man took Coyote home with him and made him work for him and his sister, and treated him very cruelly, because he had stolen his robe. One time while the man was out hunting, Coyote went into the lodge and said to the sister in a loud, angry voice: "Pack up your clothes; I am going to take you to my home as prisoner, and you will have to work there as I have worked here. Your brother is killed and now you must come with me." The girl was frightened and obeyed. They started toward Coyote's home. Coyote went behind the girl with a long stick in his hand, and whenever she stopped or fell, he hit her with the stick. The girl went on, though she was so tired and frightened, that she could hardly move as she went. She prayed that her brother was not dead, but would come and help her.

In the meantime, the man returned home and found his sister and Coyote gone. He knew at once what had happened and started after them and soon caught up with them; for he had the power to travel as fast as the fleetest arrow, though Coyote did not know it. When he was almost up with them, he shot an arrow in front of his sister. She saw it and knew that her brother was coming to help her; then she began to cry the more from joy. Coyote whipped her for crying and made her travel faster.

The man saw Coyote strike his sister and heard the cruel words that he spoke to her. He went on a hill and then shot another arrow. Coyote looked up and saw him and became frightened even more than the girl had been. He dropped his stick and ran to the girl and begged her to let him carry her bundle of clothing, and begged her not to cry. The man came down from the hill and asked Coyote where he was going with his sister. Coyote said that the people had treated them so badly he had decided to take the girl to another village, where the people would be kind to her. He said that he was helping her along the way and had been kind to her. The brother of the girl did not believe Coyote, for he had seen his treatment of her. He told Coyote to take the bundle of clothes and put it on his back; then he told his sister to sit on the bundle. He put his bow-string through Coyote's mouth and gave the ends to the girl. She sawed the strings back and forth and the man ran along by the side of Coyote, whipping him, and thus they returned to their home. This man was the Wind, who had become angry at Coyote for stealing his robe and trying to catch Deer with it, instead of waiting for him to give him power.

Turkey Makes the Corn and Coyote Plants It

(Apache)
Based on a tale reported
by Grenville Goodwin in 1939

Long ago when all the animals talked like people, Turkey overheard a boy begging his sister for food.

"What does your little brother want?" he asked the girl.

"He's hungry, but we have nothing to eat," she said.

When Turkey heard this, he shook himself all over. Many kinds of fruits and wild food dropped out of his body, and the brother and sister ate these up. Turkey shook himself again, and a variety of corn that is very large dropped out of his feathers. He shook himself a third time, and yellow corn dropped out.

And when he shook himself for the fourth time, white corn dropped out.

Bear came over, and Turkey told him, "I'm helping to feed my sister and my brother, over there."

Bear said, "You can shake only four times to make food come out of you, but I have every kind of food on me, from my feet to my head."

Bear shook himself, and out of his fur dropped juniper berries. He shook himself again, and out dropped a cactus that is good to eat. Then he shook out acorns, then another kind of cactus, then gambel oak acorns, then blue oak acorns, then pinion nuts, then a species of sumac, then manzanita berries, then wild mulberries, then saguaro fruit.

Turkey said to the boy and girl, "I have four kinds of corn seeds here for you, and this is a good place to plant them."

The sister and brother cut digging sticks and made holes with them. In the holes they planted all their corn seeds. The next day the corn had already come up and was about a foot and a half high.

The girl said, "We still have some squash seeds here," so they planted them too. The boy and girl asked Turkey for more corn seed. "The corn is coming up nicely," they said, "so we want to make another farm and plant more corn there." Turkey gave them the seed, and they left him to look after their first fields while they started off to make the other farm.

When they came back, they heard Turkey hollering at the corn field. They ran down there and saw him dragging one wing along the ground on the side toward them. There were snakes on the other side of him, and he pretended to have a broken wing to lure the snakes away and shield the boy and girl.

The squash plants had young squash on them, and the corn had grown tall and formed ears and tassels. The tassels had pollen in them, and the snakes had come to gather the pollen out of the corn plants.

Turkey told the boy and the girl to stay away from the corn for four days, when the snakes would be finished. At the end of the four days, the corn was ripe.

Turkey told them, "This will be the only time when the corn will come up in four days. From now on it will take quite a while."

And it does.

By now, the brother and sister had planted corn three times, and they gave seeds to other people. Then Slim Coyote came and asked for some.

"The corn you planted is growing well, and the ears are coming out on it," he said. "I'd like to have some seeds to plant for myself." Coyote would have to do lots of work if he wanted to raise his corn, but that wasn't his plan. "These other people here plant their corn, and after it's grown, they have to cook it. Me, I am not going to do it that way. I'll cook my corn first, and then plant it, so I won't have to bother to cook it when it's ripe."

Here's where Coyote made a big mistake. He cooked his corn, ate some, planted quite a patch of the rest. He felt pretty good about it. "Now I've done well for myself. You people have to cook your corn after you plant it, but mine will be already cooked," he said.

After planting, he went off with the rest of the people to gather acorns, but when they returned to their fields, Coyote's had nothing growing on it at all.

He said angrily, "You people must have taken the hearts out of the corn seeds you gave to me."

"No, we didn't do that," they told him, "But you cooked the heart out of them before you planted."

Coyote asked for more seeds and planted them the right way this time. So, his corn grew: the day after he planted it, it was up about a foot and a half. He felt good. The people who had planted their corn at the beginning were harvesting now and tying it up into bundles. Coyote saw these and wanted some. People got mad at Coyote because he was always asking them for corn.

"I just want some green ears to feed my children," he would say. "As soon as my corn is ripe, I'll pay you back."

The other people had all their corn in and stripped now, but their squashes were still growing in the field. Coyote stole their squash, and the people all came to his camp. They wanted to know if he was the one who was stealing their squash.

Coyote pretended to get angry. "You're always blaming me for stealing everything. There are lots of camps over there. Why do you choose mine to come to with your accusations?"

But the people knew about Coyote's thieving ways. "From now on, don't make your farm near us. Move away and live someplace else!" they said.

"All right. There are several of you that I was going to repay with corn, but I won't do it now that you've treated me this way," he said. So, Coyote's family lived poorly, and they never bothered to cook anything before they ate it.

Coyote and Sun

(Paiute)
Katharine Berry Judson, Myths and Legends of California and the Old Southwest, 1912

Along time ago, Coyote wanted to go to the sun. He asked Pokoh, Old Man, to show him the trail. Coyote went straight out on this trail and he traveled it all day.

But Sun went round so that Coyote came back at night to the place from which he started in the morning.

The next morning, Coyote asked Pokoh to show him the trail. Pokoh showed him, and Coyote traveled all day and came back at night to the same place again.

But the third day, Coyote started early and went out on the trail to the edge of the world and sat down on the hole where the sun came up. While waiting for the sun he pointed with his bow and arrow at different places and pretended to shoot. He also pretended not to see the sun. When Sun came up, he told Coyote to get out of his way.

Coyote told him to go around; that it was his trail. But Sun came up under him and he had to hitch forward a little. After Sun came up a little farther, it began to get hot on Coyote's shoulder, so he spit on his paw and rubbed his shoulder.

Then he wanted to ride up with the sun. Sun said, "Oh, no"; but Coyote insisted. So, Coyote climbed up on Sun, and Sun started up the trail in the sky. The trail was marked off into steps like a ladder. As Sun went up, he counted "one, two, three," and so on. By and by Coyote became very thirsty, and he asked Sun for a drink of water.

Sun gave him an acorn-cup full. Coyote asked him why he had no more. About noontime, Coyote became very impatient. It was very hot. Sun told him to shut his eyes. Coyote shut them, but opened them again. He kept opening and shutting them all the afternoon.

At night, when Sun came down, Coyote took hold of a tree. Then he clambered off Sun and climbed down to the earth.

Skunk Outwits Coyote

*Native American
Source Unknown*

Coyote was going along one day, feeling very hungry, when he met up with Skunk. "Hello, brother," Coyote greeted him. "You look hungry and so am I. If I lead the way, will you join me in a trick to get something to eat?"

"I will do whatever you propose," said Skunk.

"A prairie dog village is just over that hill. You go over there and lie down and play dead. I'll come along later and say to the prairie dogs, 'Come, let us have a dance over the body of our dead enemy.' "

Skunk wondered how they would ever get anything to eat by playing dead and dancing. "Why should I do this?" he asked. "Go on," Coyote said. "Puff yourself up and play dead."

Skunk went on to the prairie dog village and pretended to be dead. After a while Coyote came along and saw several prairie dogs playing outside their holes. They were keeping a distance between themselves and Skunk.

"Oh, look," cried Coyote, "our enemy lies dead before us. Come, we will have a dance to celebrate. Let everyone come out and then stop up the burrow holes."

The foolish prairie dogs did as he told them. "Now," said Coyote, "let us all stand in a big circle and dance with our eyes closed. If anyone opens his eyes to look, he will turn into something bad."

As soon as the prairie dogs began dancing with their eyes closed, Coyote killed one of them. "Well, now," he called out, "let's all open our eyes." The prairie dogs did so, and were surprised to see one lying dead. "Oh, dear," said Coyote, "look at this poor fellow. He opened his eyes and died. Now, all of you, close your eyes and dance again. Don't look, or you too will die."

They began to dance once more, and one by one Coyote drew them out of the dance circle and killed them. At last, one of the prairie dogs became suspicious and opened his eyes. "Oh, Coyote is killing us!" he cried, and all the survivors ran to unstop their holes and seek safety in the burrows.

Skunk then stood up, laughing at how easily Coyote had worked his trick. He helped gather up some dry firewood and they began roasting the prairie dogs that Coyote had killed.

The cooking meat smelled so good that Coyote decided he wanted to eat the best of it himself. "Let's run a race," he said. "The one that wins will have his choice of the most delicious prairie dogs."

"No," replied Skunk, "you are too swift. I'm a slow runner and can never beat you."

"Well, I will tie a rock to my foot," Coyote said.

"If you will tie on a big rock, I will race you."

They decided to race around the bottom of the hill. "While I am tying this rock to my foot," Coyote said, "you go ahead. I'll give you a start and then catch you."

Skunk began to run and was soon out of sight around the hill. Coyote tied a rock to his foot and followed, slowly at first, but he soon kicked the rock loose and doubled his speed. Along the way, however, Skunk had found a brush pile, and he dashed in there and hid.

As soon as he saw Coyote go racing past, Skunk turned back to the fire. He raked all the roasted prairie dogs out of the coals, except for two small bony ones that he did not want. Then he cut off the tails and stuck them back in the ashes, and carried the meat away to the brush pile.

Meanwhile Coyote was still loping around the hill, confident that Skunk was running just ahead of him. As he hurried along, he said to himself, "I wonder where that fool Skunk is? I did not know that he could run so fast." He soon circled back to the cooking fire and saw the prairie dog tails sticking out of the ashes. He seized one and it slipped out. He tried another one. "Oh, but they are well cooked," he said. He tried another one. Then he suspected that something was wrong.

Taking a stick, Coyote raked through the coals, but he found only the two bony prairie dogs that Skunk had rejected. "Someone must have stolen our meat," he said, and then ate the two small tasteless ones.

Skunk, who by this time had feasted on the delicious meat, had crept to the top of the hill and was looking down at Coyote. As Coyote began searching all around to see who might have stolen the meat, Skunk threw some prairie dog bones down upon him.

Coyote glanced up and saw him. "You took all the delicious prairie dogs!" he cried. "Give me some of them."

"No," Skunk answered. "We ran a race for them. I beat you. I'm going to eat all of them."

Coyote begged and begged for some of the delicious prairie dogs, but while he was still pleading, Skunk swallowed the last morsel of meat. He was a better trickster than Coyote.

Coyote's Salmon

(Sanpoils)

Long ago on the Sanpoil River that flows southward into the Columbia River, Old Man and Old Woman lived with their tribe, the Sanpoils. They were so stooped that it appeared they were walking on their knees and their elbows. Their very pretty granddaughter lived with them.

One day Coyote came along and saw the old couple with the beautiful girl. Immediately, he decided that he wanted the girl for his wife. But he knew better than to ask for her then. He thought he would wait until evening. So, during the day he sat around, becoming better acquainted with the family.

The old couple watched him, noting that his long hair was braided neatly and his forelocks were carefully combed back. They noticed too that he was tall and strong. Old Man and Old Woman talked between themselves about Coyote, wondering if he could be a Chief.

In the late afternoon, Coyote asked Old Man, "What is that thing down in the stream?"

"Why, that is my fish trap," Old Man replied.

"A fish trap? What is that? What do you do with it?" asked Coyote, pretending he did not know.

"Oh, occasionally I catch a few bullheads and sunfish," Old Man said.

"Is that what you eat? I never heard of them. Are they big enough for a meal?" asked Coyote.

"They are not much, but what else can we eat?" replied Old Man.

"I think I will go up the hill and look around," said Coyote. It was then about an hour before sunset.

On top of the hill, Coyote saw some grouse roosting in a tree. He threw some stones at them, killing five. He carried the grouse back to Old Man and said, "Let's eat these for supper."

After removing the feathers, Old Man roasted the game over the fire and when they were done, everyone sat down to eat the wonderful meal. To Old Man and his family, it seemed like a feast.

"Is this the kind of food you eat every day?" the Old Man asked Coyote.

"Sometimes I eat berries, roots, and I catch some real big fish, as long as your arm," Coyote said.

Later, Coyote announced that he would like to stay there if they wanted him, otherwise he would move on.

"What do you mean?" asked Old Man.

"Well, it is like this. I would like to marry your granddaughter," said Coyote.

Old Man and Old Woman looked at each other but said nothing. Coyote went for a little walk to allow the old couple to talk privately.

While Coyote was gone Old Man said to his wife, "What do you think of this fellow? You saw what he did, bringing good food for our supper. If we let him marry our granddaughter, maybe they will stay here and we will have such good food always. Surely our girl will marry someone soon; perhaps some man not as good as this young fellow."

"Well, husband, I'll leave it entirely up to you."

Soon Coyote returned. He decided to let Old Man open the conversation. Old Man held his pipe in one hand and said, "How I wish I had a smoke. My tobacco ran out some time ago."

"Have some of mine," said Coyote, reaching into his jacket pocket. He pulled out a large bunch of tobacco and gave it to Old Man, who filled his pipe, feeling very much surprised that Coyote would have real tobacco.

After a while Old Man spoke, "My wife and I have talked over your proposal and she left the decision up to me. I have decided to let you marry our granddaughter and live here. If you go away, we do not want you to take her with you. How are we to know that you will do this?"
"You need not worry," said Coyote. "I am tired of travelling. I want to settle down here for the rest of my life, if you wish."

Old Man was pleased with Coyote and believed what he said. So, Coyote took the pretty granddaughter for his wife.

Early that evening Coyote stayed with his wife and later said, "I am going out for a few minutes and when I return, we will go to bed."

"All right," answered his wife.

Coyote went downstream to where Old Man had his fish trap. He changed it into a basket-type trap, piling rows of rocks to guide fish into the basket. When finished he called out, "Salmon, I want two of you in the basket trap tomorrow morning, one male and one female." Then he returned to his bride.

Next morning Coyote asked Old Man to go to his fish trap early. "I think I heard a noise in the night that sounded like fish caught in a trap," he said.

Old Man went downstream to see his fish trap. Sure enough, he saw two big fish in the trap. Old Man was so excited, he stumbled up the trail toward Coyote.

"You were right, there are two great fish in the trap bigger than I have ever seen," reported Old Man.

"You must be dreaming," said Coyote.

"Come down with me and see for yourself," Old Man said.

When the two reached the trap, Coyote exclaimed, "You are so right. These are salmon, chief among all fish. Let us take them over to that flat place, and I will show you what to do with them."

When they reached the open field, Coyote sent Old Man up the hill to gather sunflower stems and leaves.

"Those are salmon plants," Coyote explained. "Salmon must always be laid on sunflower stems and leaves."

Old Man spread the sunflower plants upon the ground. Coyote placed the salmon on them, and proceeded to show Old Man how to prepare the salmon.

"First, put a stick in the salmon's mouth and bend it back to break off the head. Second, place long sharp poles inside the salmon lengthwise to hold for roasting over your campfire," said Coyote.

"Now remember this," he continued. "The first week go down to the trap and take out the salmon every day. But when fixing it, never use a knife to cut it in any way. Always roast the fish over the fire on sticks, the way I have shown you. Never boil salmon the first week. After the salmon is roasted, open it carefully and take out the backbone without breaking it. Also, save the back part of the head for the sacred bundle-never eat that.

"If you do not do these things as I have told you, either a big storm will come up and you will be drowned, or you will be bitten by a rattlesnake and you will die.

"After you have taken out the salmon's backbone, wrap it and the back of the head carefully in tules, the marsh grasses, to make a sacred bundle, then place it somewhere in a tree, where it will not be bothered. If you do as I tell you, you will always have plenty of salmon in your trap.

"I am telling you these sacred things about the salmon because I am going to die sometime. I want you and your tribe to know of the best way to care for and use your salmon. After this, your men will always place their fish traps up and down the river to catch salmon. The man having the first trap will be Chief of the Salmon, and the others should always do anything he tells them to do.

"After the first week of the salmon season, you can boil your salmon or cook it any way you wish. But remember to always take care of the bones, wrapping them in a sacred bundle--never leaving them where they can be stepped upon or stepped over."

For the next few days each time Old Man went down to his fish trap in the morning, he found twice as many salmon as on the day before. Coyote showed him how to dry fish to prepare them for winter use. Before long they had a large scaffold covered with drying fish.

People of the Sanpoil tribe saw the fish and noticed how well Old Man and Old Woman were doing. They went to their hogans and told others about the big red fish called salmon, and about the tall young stranger who taught Old Man about caring for the salmon.

Soon thereafter, all the people came to see for themselves. Old Man and Old Woman invited them to feast on their roasted salmon. The old couple explained how their new grandson-in-law had shown them how to trap the salmon and dry them for winter food.

To this day, the Sanpoils say their tribe harvests the salmon in exactly the way that Coyote taught their ancestors long, long ago.

Iktomi and the Coyote

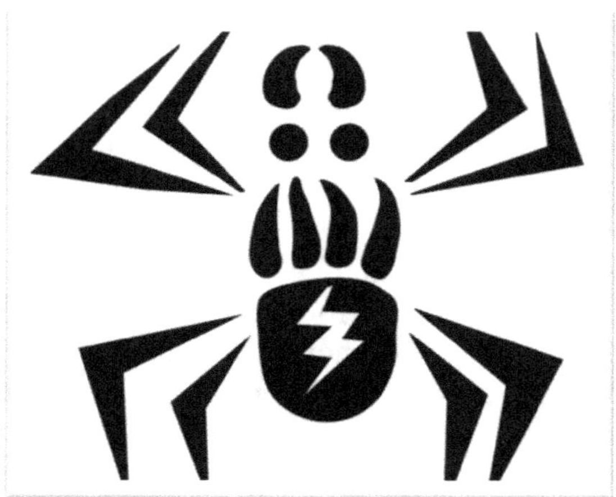

A far off upon a large level land, a summer sun was shining bright. Here and there over the rolling green were tall bunches of coarse gray weeds. Iktomi in his fringed buckskins walked alone across the prairie with a black bare head glossy in the sunlight. He walked through the grass without following any well-worn footpath.

From one large bunch of coarse weeds to another he wound his way about the great plain. He lifted his foot lightly and placed it gently forward like a wildcat prowling noiselessly through the thick grass. He stopped a few steps away from a very large bunch of wild sage. From shoulder to shoulder he tilted his head. Still farther he bent from side to side, first low over one hip and then over the other. Far forward he stooped, stretching his long thin neck like a duck, to see what lay under a fur coat beyond the bunch of coarse grass.

A sleek gray-faced prairie wolf! his pointed black nose tucked in between his four feet drawn snugly together; his handsome bushy tail wound over his nose and feet; a coyote fast asleep in the shadow of a bunch of grass! -- this is what Iktomi spied. Carefully he raised one foot and cautiously reached out with his toes. Gently, gently he lifted the foot behind and placed it before the other. Thus, he came nearer and nearer to the round fur ball lying motionless under the sage grass.

Now Iktomi stood beside it, looking at the closed eyelids that did not quiver the least bit. Pressing his lips into straight lines and nodding his head slowly, he bent over the wolf. He held his ear close to the coyote's nose, but not a breath of air stirred from it.

"Dead!" said he at last. "Dead, but not long since he ran over these plains! See! there in his paw is caught a fresh feather. He is nice fat meat!" Taking hold of the paw with the bird feather fast on it, he exclaimed, "Why, he is still warm! I'll carry him to my dwelling and have a roast for my evening meal. Ah-ha!" he laughed, as he seized the coyote by its two fore paws and its two hind feet and swung him over head across his shoulders. The wolf was large and the teepee was far across the prairie. Iktomi trudged along with his burden, smacking his hungry lips together. He blinked his eyes hard to keep out the salty perspiration streaming down his face.

All the while the coyote on his back lay gazing into the sky with wide open eyes. His long white teeth fairly gleamed as he smiled and smiled.

"To ride on one's own feet is tiresome, but to be carried like a warrior from a brave fight is great fun!" said the coyote in his heart. He had never been borne on any one's back before and the new experience delighted him. He lay there lazily on Iktomi's shoulders, now and then blinking blue winks. Did you never see a birdie blink a blue wink? This is how it first became a saying among the plains people. When a bird stands aloof watching your strange ways, a thin bluish white tissue slips quickly over his eyes and as quickly off again; so quick that you think it was only a mysterious blue wink. Sometimes when children grow drowsy, they blink blue winks, while others who are too proud to look with friendly eyes upon people blink in this cold bird-manner.

The coyote was affected by both sleepiness and pride. His winks were almost as blue as the sky. In the midst of his new pleasure the swaying motion ceased. Iktomi had reached his dwelling place. The coyote felt drowsy no longer, for in the next instant he was slipping out of Iktomi's hands. He was falling, falling through space, and then he struck the ground with such a bump he did not wish to breathe for a while. He wondered what Iktomi would do, thus he lay still where he fell. Humming a dance-song, one from his bundle of mystery songs, Iktomi hopped and darted about at an imaginary dance and feast. He gathered dry willow sticks and broke them in two against his knee. He built a large fire out of doors. The flames leaped up high in red and yellow streaks. Now Iktomi returned to the coyote who had been looking on through his eyelashes.

Taking him again by his paws and hind feet, he swung him to and fro. Then as the wolf swung toward the red flames, Iktomi let him go. Once again, the coyote fell through space. Hot air smote his nostrils. He saw red dancing fire, and now he struck a bed of cracking embers. With a quick turn he leaped out of the flames. From his heels were scattered a shower of red coals upon Iktomi's bare arms and shoulders. Dumfounded, Iktomi thought he saw a spirit walk out of his fire. His jaws fell apart. He thrust a palm to his face, hard over his mouth! He could scarce keep from shrieking.

Rolling over and over on the grass and rubbing the sides of his head against the ground, the coyote soon put out the fire on his fur. Iktomi's eyes were almost ready to jump out of his head as he stood cooling a burn on his brown arm with his breath.

Sitting on his haunches, on the opposite side of the fire from where Iktomi stood, the coyote began to laugh at him.

"Another day, my friend, do not take too much for granted. Make sure the enemy is stone dead before you make a fire!"

Then off he ran so swiftly that his long bushy tail hung out in a straight line with his back.

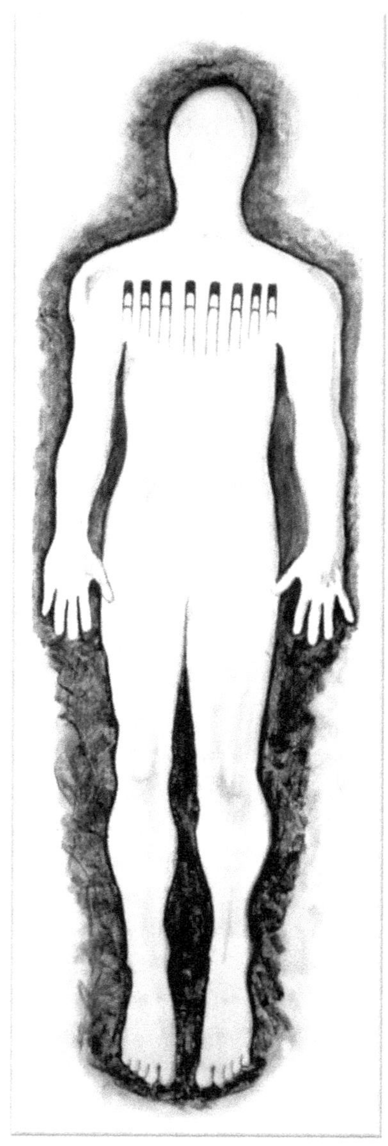

Creation Myth

(Maidu)
Roland B. Dixon,
Publications of the
American Ethnological
Society Volume IV, 1912

When this world was filled with water, Earth-Maker floated upon it, kept floating about. Nowhere in the world could he see even a tiny bit of earth. No persons of any kind flew about. He went about in this world, the world itself being invisible, transparent like the sky.

He was troubled. "I wonder how, I wonder where, I wonder in what place, in what country, we shall find a world!" he said.

"You are a very strong man, to be thinking of this world," said Coyote.

"I am guessing in what direction the world is, then to that distant land let us float!" said Earth-Maker.

In this world they kept floating along, kept floating along, hungry, having nothing to eat. "You will die of hunger," said Coyote. Then he thought. "No, I cannot think of anything," he said.

"Well," said Earth-Maker, "the world is large, a great world. If somewhere I find a tiny world, I can fix it up."

Then he sang, "Where, little world, art thou?" It is said he sang, kept singing, sang all the time. "Enough!" he said, and stopped singing. "Well! I don't know many songs," he said.

Then Coyote sang again, kept singing, asking, for the world, singing, "Where, O world, art thou.'"

He sang, kept singing; then "Enough!" he said, "I am tired. You try again."

So, Earth-Maker sang. "Where are you, my great mountains, my world mountains?" he said. He sang, and all the time kept saying, "Where are you?" He stopped singing. "Enough!" he said. "You try also."

Coyote tried, kept singing. "My foggy mountains, where one goes about," he said. "Well, we shall see nothing at all. I guess there never was a world anywhere," said he.

"I think if we find a little world, I can fix it very well," said Earth-Maker.

As they floated along, they saw something like a bird's nest. "Well! That is very small," said Earth-Maker. "It is small. If it were larger, I could fix it. But it is too small," he said. "I wonder how I can stretch it a little!" He kept saying, "What is the best way! How shall I make it larger?" So, saying, he prepared it. He extended a rope to the east, to the south he extended a rope, to the west, to the northwest, and to the north he extended ropes.

When all were stretched, he said, "Well, sing, you who were the finder of this earth, this mud! 'In the long, long, ago, Robin-Man made the world, stuck earth together, making this world.' Thus, mortal men shall say of you, in myth-telling." Then Robin sang, and his world-making song sounded sweet. After the ropes were all stretched, he kept singing; then, after a time, he ceased.

Then Earth-Maker spoke to Coyote also. "Do you sing too," he said. So, he sang, singing, "My world, where one travels by the valley-edge; my world of many foggy mountains; my world where one goes zigzagging hither and thither; range after range," he said, "I sing of the country I shall travel in. In such a world I shall wander," he said.

Then Earth-Maker sang--sang of the world he had made, kept singing, until by and by, he ceased. "Now," he said, "it would be well if the world were a little larger. Let us stretch it!"--"Stop!" said Coyote. I speak wisely. This world ought to be painted with something, so that it may look pretty. What do ye two think?"

Then Robin-Man said, "I am one who knows nothing. Ye two are clever men, making this world, talking it over; if ye find anything evil, ye will make it good."

"Very well," said Coyote, "I will paint it with blood. There shall be blood in the world; and people shall be born there, having blood. There shall be birds born who shall have blood. Everything--deer, all kinds of game, all sorts of men without any exception--all things shall have blood that are to be created in this world. And in another place, making it red, there shall be red rocks. It will be as if blood were mixed up with the world, and thus the world will be beautiful," he said.

"What do you think about it?"

"Your words are good," he said, "I know nothing."

So, Robin-Man went off. As he went, he said, "I shall be a person who travels only in this way," and he flew away.

Earth-Maker spoke: "You had better lie down here on your face."--"All right!" said Coyote, and, kneeling down, he lay on his face. Then Earth-Maker stretched the world with his foot. Stretching it once, he extended it towards the east, extended it on that side; then to the south, then to the west, he stretched it; then to the northwest and to the north he stretched it. Having extended it only a little ways, he said, "All right!"

Coyote stood up and looked around. "Well, I think it would be better if this world were just large enough to go around it." By and by Earth-Maker said, "You had better kneel down again, and lie flat on your belly. Do not look up. You must not!" "Very well," said Coyote, "I will not look up." He lay down; and Earth-Maker, stretching the earth with his foot eastward, stretched it as far as it would go. He extended it fully toward the south, toward the west, toward the northwest, toward the north. "All right!" said he.

Coyote stood up, and, having risen, started to walk hither eastward. Earth-Maker, when he was left alone, stood for a time, then, departing, he went toward the south. In the direction of the sunset, he went far around, going over to the northwest, going around to the north, going all the way around to the east. And having gone around, having returned to the spot where he had first turned off, he prepared things.

He made two white men; then he made others, white, but a little different. As he made them, he counted them. He kept on making them--made one black, then another almost black. Two of each only he made. Then he counted all the countries, and, as he counted, assigned them, gave them to the countries. "You are a country having this name, you shall have this people," he said.

"This sort of people, naming you, shall own the country. These people shall grow, shall keep on growing through many winters, through many dawns. They shall continue to grow until, their appointed winters being past, their dawns being over, this people having finished growing, shall be born," he said.

"Very many winters will have passed before they shall be born. And they shall have children, girls and boys; and these children, growing up, shall have children in their turn," he said. When several winters have passed, there will be very many people."

Then again, to another sort of people, he gave another country, saying, "This people, I leave you in this country, and ye shall be the owners of this land. Ye shall be a people with a name."

And they also were a different sort of people, a people with a name; and their country also was named, it is said.

"Your country also shall have a name," he said. "Ye too shall have a name, and your children shall fill the land, and every single child shall have a name," he said. "There, growing steadily, many winters, many days, shall pass before ye are fully grown. Then ye shall possess this country," he said.

Thereafter he spoke to another; again, he gave a different kind of country to a different kind of people. He said, "Ye shall be a different-speaking and a different-looking people. Ye also shall possess a country," he said.

"Your children, if they weary of this land, going from this country to one with another name, to a country that is good to live in, shall remain there. There every country shall be full of people, who will continue to be born," he said.

And then he divided the world among many. To one he gave one sort, to another he gave another. Ye shall all have different names," he said. Finally, he finished giving, he distributed all.

Then after a while, continuing on his way, he came hither, kept traveling; and after arriving in the middle of the world, he made other people. "Ye shall be mortal men like this," he said; and, having made two, he left them. "Ye here, growing steadily, when so many winters shall have passed, very many winters, many days, ye shall be fully grown," he said.

"Then ye shall be mortal men, ye shall be born full-grown. This country shall have a name.

Beyond these mountains there shall be another country, which also shall have a name. Ye shall not be born soon," he said. Then he named everything, and, having left the people here in the middle of the world, he went away.

Continuing on his way, he went to all countries that were of the proper sort; and when he had gone as far as mortal men were to live, he stopped.

Then there again he created two--two more, it is said, he lay down, and again two more.

He kept counting them; and when he had counted them all, he spoke. "Ye shall remain here," he said, "and your country shall have a name. Although living in a small country, in one that is not large, it shall be sufficient for you. This I leave; and growing continually, so many winters passing, very many winters passing, many days passing, ye shall be fully grown. And then ye, being fully grown, shall be born," he said.

"Then your food will grow, --different sorts of food, all kinds of food; and ye, being born with sufficient intelligence, will survive," he said. Then he pushed them down under a gopher-hill.

He spoke again. "Ye, too, shall possess a small country. 'Come, now! leave this country!' (This ye must not say to others, wishing to take their land.) Ye shall be people who will not drive others away, driving them off to another country. Ye shall be different, ye shall name your country. Ye also shall be a differently named people. There, growing continually, many days being passed, many winters having passed, ye shall be born, when your birthday has passed," he said.

"Living there and having children, when other winters are passed, they will become a little larger, and will keep on thus, growing all the time, until, when enough winters shall have passed, always becoming more numerous, ye shall have enough people. Your children, all without exception, shall have names. This country also, in the same way is named; all countries shall have names, just as yourselves. If ye are going to look at the country over there, then, when ye go, (ye shall say) 'I am going to that place,' naming it;

then all people will understand where ye are going," he said.

Then, counting the people on this side (in this direction), he left them; and, speaking to those on this side, he said, "Ye also shall be mortal men. So many winters passing over, ye shall be born. All the time growing, each winter ye shall grow a little, a very little. Again, when the winter is over, continually growing, when many winters are passed, ye will have finished growing; then ye shall be born, full-grown. There ye also shall have a country, and your country shall be one bearing a name, and ye too shall be named," he said.

"Ye shall have children; and when your children have grown larger, then, looking all over this country, ye must tell them about it, teach them about it, naming the country and places, showing them and naming them to your children. 'That is such and such a place, and that is such and such a mountain.' So, when ye have caused them to learn this, teaching them, they shall understand even as ye do yourselves." Then, placing them between his thumb and finger, he snapped them away.

And when he had given countries thus to all that he had counted out, there was one pair left. "Ye also, ye shall be a, people speaking differently. There will be a little too many of you for you to have the same sort of a country also. So ye shall have that kind of a country, a great country," he said.

"Now, wherever I have passed along, there shall never be a lack of anything," he said, and made motions in all directions.

"The country where I have been shall be one where nothing

is ever lacking. I have finished talking to you, and I say to you that ye shall remain where ye are to be born. Ye are the last people; and while, ye are to remain where ye are created, I shall return, and stay there. When this world becomes bad, I will make it over again; and after I make it, ye shall be born," he said. Long ago Coyote suspected this, they say.

"This world will shake," he said. "This world is spread out flat, the world is not stable. After this world is all made, by and by, after a long time, I will pull this rope a little, then the world shall be firm. I, pulling on my rope, shall make it shake. And now," he said, "there shall be songs, they shall not be lacking, ye shall have them."

And he sang, and kept on singing until he ceased singing. "Ye mortal men shall have this song," he said, and then he sang another; and singing many different songs, he walked along, kept walking until he reached the middle of the world; and there, sitting down over across from it, he remained.

But, in making the world, Robin-Man sang that which was pleasant to hear. He, they say, was the first created person, --a man whose song passed across the valleys, a man who found the world, a man who in the olden time sang very beautifully-sounding songs.

And Earth-Maker, going along, and having passed by the middle of the world, made a house for himself, and remained there. That is as far as he went. That is all, they say.

Adventures of Coyote

(A Cougar Tale)
(Caddo)
Dorsey, George A.
Traditions of the Caddo.
Washington: Carnegie Institution. 1905

In the beginning of the world there were many, many people, and the people held councils to decide how things should be. There was one man, named Coyote, who always had something to say on every subject.

At one council this question came up: "How and what kind of rain should be in the world?" One of the men said that it should rain in the form of lead balls, which would be very dangerous, and so when the rain came the people would have to stay at home. Then Coyote arose from his seat and said: "If it should rain nothing but lead it would be very dangerous for my people, because they do not stay at home very much, and as for myself, I might be carrying a big deer to my family to eat when the rain begins to fall and I would certainly be killed. I say, let it rain in drops of water.

Then we can be caught out in the rain and get very wet, but we will soon be dry again, and the wetting will be good for us." The people accepted Coyote's suggestion, and so it is that it rains in the form of water.

When the council was all over and the people went to their homes, Coyote made up his mind to go out and visit some of his friends. He traveled until he came to the mountains. He saw smoke coming up among the mountains, as though some one was making up a big fire, and he thought he would go up and see who was living there.

When he came near to the place, he saw some one sitting by the fire. It was the great, powerful Bear. Coyote went closer, and Bear asked him if he was the person who was called Coyote, and Bear told him that if he was that he was going to kill him, for he had heard many bad things about him. Coyote told Bear he was not the person, but that he was the son of a great and powerful medicine-man. Bear did not believe him and decided to kill him.

When he was about to kill him, Coyote told him to wait until his father saw him, for he might have something to say to him before he died. This happened at sunrise, and when the sun was just peeping over the hilltops Coyote said to Bear: "Now you may kill me or do as you please with me, because my father is watching me." Then Bear began to back away, and as he did so, Coyote began to go nearer and nearer to Bear.

Finally, he began to push him with his elbow, at the same time saying: "Now kill me while my father is watching me." Bear thought that he must be a great man, if he was the son of the Sun, and he wondered how he received his powers from the Sun. He became frightened and gave Coyote many things to eat, and then Coyote told Bear to come and make him a visit some time, whenever he felt like going anywhere. A long while after this, Bear found out that the person who made a visit to him was not the son of the Sun, but that he was the man Coyote, whom he wanted to kill. Bear was angrier at him than ever, and so he thought he would fool Coyote some way by going and visiting him and killing him if he could find his home. Bear did not find his home, because Coyote was always moving from place to place, for he knew that Bear was after him, and that he would kill him if he could catch him.

While Coyote was moving from one place to another he came down to a large lake of clear, cool water, and after he had been there for some time, he started off a little way from the lake. While gone he saw some one coming up toward him and, as he was very cowardly, he started to run away. The person was not his enemy, but a friend of his, Mountain-Lion. He called Coyote back, and so he came, and he told his friend that he was very hungry, for he had had nothing to eat for a long while. Mountain-Lion asked him to go along with him, saying that he would find something for him to eat soon.

They both went to the lake, and when they came down to the water Mountain-Lion told Coyote that he was going to kill a young horse. In those times there were many herds of wild horses, and at the lake there was a certain place where the wild horses drank. Near the place where the road led to the water there was a large tree, and the horses passed under the tree as they went down to the water.

Every day at about noon Mountain-Lion would climb the tree and then pounce down on a young horse and kill him. As Mountain-Lion and Coyote drew near to the tree Mountain-Lion told Coyote to place himself where the wild herd of horses could not see him, and so he did, and Mountain-Lion climbed the tree.

Soon Coyote saw dust rise up from the ground and he heard something like thundering, and later he saw many hundreds of horses coming down to the water. As the horses were passing under the tree, Coyote saw Mountain-Lion jump out of the tree and pounce upon a young horse and kill it. Then Mountain-Lion and Coyote both had a fine dinner.

That day, after they had eaten, Mountain-Lion told Coyote to continue on his way; but Coyote did not want to leave his friend, and so he asked Mountain-Lion if he could give him power so that he could kill a horse, too, and eat it when he was hungry. Mountain-Lion told him he would.

They stayed there until the next day, and at about noon they both went down to the lake again, and went to the tree, and then Mountain-Lion showed Coyote how and what to do when the horses should come. He taught him how to climb the tree, and then he went out to place himself where the horses could not see him.

Soon they began to come from different directions, and as they filed down to the water Coyote picked out a fat young horse, and as they were coming up from the water, he jumped on it and killed it. They had another fine dinner, and then Mountain-Lion said to Coyote: "Do not try to kill a three or four-year-old horse. If you jump on one that is three years old you cannot kill him and you may lose your own life. Try to kill one that is one or two years old and you will succeed every time."

Coyote left his new friend and went on his way. The next day, while he was alone, he began to get very hungry, and so at about noon he went down to the lake to kill a horse. While he was on the tree, he said to himself: "I wonder if it would be dangerous for me to kill one of the large horses. I may be stronger than Mountain-Lion, and so I will try to kill the largest horse and I will show Mountain-Lion that I am not so small as I look to him."

The horses began to go down to the water, and Coyote waited and waited for the chance to jump upon the largest horse in the herd. Finally, a large horse came, and when he was right under the tree Coyote jumped upon him.

It was but a short time until the horse threw Coyote off from his back, and when Coyote was down on the ground the horse kicked him under the jaws and went off. As Coyote was about to die, Mountain-Lion, who had been watching Coyote all the time, came up to see what was the matter with him, and when he came up to him, he saw his jaws to one side.

Mountain-Lion asked Coyote what he was laughing about, and asked him if he was able to kill another five-year-old horse. Coyote lay there for a long time before he was able to move. Finally, he arose and decided to leave the place, never to return to it.

As he was going along a small stream, he heard some one up in a persimmon tree, and so he thought that he would go over and see who it was. He found Opossum in the persimmon tree eating persimmons. Coyote went under the tree and asked Opossum to throw down some persimmons to him. Opossum refused and laughed at Coyote and began to play with him. Opossum would take one persimmon and eat it, and then he would throw the seeds down to Coyote.

Finally, Coyote became angry at Opossum and wished he could get him down from the tree. Sometimes Opossum would get on a small limb of the tree, and then drop down as though he was going to fall to the ground, but he would always catch himself by wrapping his tail around the limb.

He kept on doing this to torment Coyote for a long time, until he climbed out on a dry limb. He threw himself off the limb again and said to Coyote: "I am falling off, sure. I am coming down," and just as he let himself off of the limb it broke off and down came Opossum. Coyote was upon him and gave him a good beating, and then he left him to die.

Opossum fooled Coyote, for he was not hurt at all, and when Coyote went away Opossum jumped up and climbed the persimmon tree again. After a while Coyote looked back to see if Opossum was dead. He could not see him, and so he went back and found that Opossum was gone. He looked up in the tree, and there he saw him laughing at him again.

The Creation

(Maidu)
Dixon, Bulletin of the American Museum of Natural History, xvii, 39, No. 1

In the beginning there was no sun, no moon, no stars. All was dark, and everywhere there was only water. A raft came floating on the water. It came from the north, and in it were two persons; Turtle and Father-of-the-Secret-Society.

The stream flowed very rapidly. Then from the sky a rope of feathers, was let down, and down it came Earth-Initiate.

When he reached the end of the rope, he tied it to the bow of the raft, and stepped in. His face was covered and was never seen, but his body shone like the sun. He sat down, and for a long time said nothing.

At last Turtle said, "Where do you come from?" and earth Initiate answered, "I come from above."

Then Turtle said, "Brother, can you not make for me some good dry land so that I may sometimes come up out of the water?"

Then he asked another time, "Are there going to be any

people in the world?"

Earth-Initiate thought awhile, then said, "Yes."

Turtle asked, "How long before you are going to make people?"

Earth-Initiate replied, "I don't know. You want to have some dry land: well, how am I going to get any earth to make it of?"

Turtle answered, "If you will tie a rock about my left arm, I'll dive for some."

Earth-Initiate did as Turtle asked, and then, reaching around, took the end of a rope from somewhere, and tied it to Turtle. When Earth-Initiate came to the raft, there was no rope there: he just reached out and found one.

Turtle said, "If the rope is not long enough, I'll jerk it once, and you must haul me up; if it is long enough, I'll give two jerks, and then you must pull me up quickly, as I shall have all the earth that I can carry." Just as Turtle went over the side of the boat, Father-of-the-Secret-Society began to shout loudly.

Turtle was gone a long time. He was gone six years; and when he came up, he was covered with green slime, he had been down so long. When he reached the top of the water, the only earth he had was a very little under his nails: the rest had all washed away. Earth-Initiate took with his right hand a stone knife from under his left armpit, and carefully scraped the earth out from under Turtle's nails.

He put the earth in the palm of his hand, and rolled it about till it was round; it was as large as a small pebble. He laid it on the stern of the raft. By and by he went to look at it: it had not grown at all. The third time that he went to look at it, it had grown so that it could be spanned by the arms. The fourth time he looked, it was as big as the world, the raft was aground, and all around were mountains as far as he could see.

The raft came ashore at Ta'doikö, and the place can be seen to-day.

When the raft had come to land, Turtle said, "I can't stay in the dark all the time. Can't you make a light, so that I can see?"

Earth-Initiate replied, "Let us get out of the raft, and then we will see what we can do." So, all three got out. Then Earth-Initiate said, "Look that way, to the east! I am going to tell my sister to come up." Then it began to grow light, and day began to break; then Father-of-the-Secret-Society began to shout loudly, and the sun came up.

Turtle said, "Which way is the sun going to travel?" Earth-Initiate answered, "I'll tell her to go this way, and go down there." After the sun went down, Father-of-the-Secret-Society began to cry and shout again, and it grew very dark.

Earth-Initiate said, "I'll tell my brother to come up." Then the moon rose. Then Earth-Initiate asked Turtle and Father-of-the-Secret-Society, "How do you like it?" and they both answered, "It is very good." Then Turtle asked, "Is that all you are going to do for us?"

Earth-Initiate answered, "No, I am going to do more yet." Then he called the stars each by its name, and they came out.

When this was done, Turtle asked, "Now what shall we

do?"

Earth-Initiate replied, "Wait, and I'll show you." Then he made a tree grow at Ta'doikö, -the tree called Hu'kiimtsa; and Earth-Initiate and Turtle and Father-of-the-Secret-Society sat in its shade for two days. The tree was very large, and had twelve different kinds of acorns growing on it.

After they had sat for two days under the tree, they all went off to see the world that Earth-Initiate had made. They started at sunrise, and were back by sunset. Earth-Initiate traveled so fast that all they could see was a ball of fire flashing about under the ground and the water. While they were gone, Coyote and his dog Rattlesnake came up out of the ground. It is said that Coyote could see Earth-Initiate's face.

When Earth-Initiate and the others came back, they found Coyote at Ta'doikö. All five of them then built huts for themselves, and lived there at Ta'doikö, but no one could go inside of Earth-Initiate's house. Soon after the travelers came back, Earth-Initiate called the birds from the air, and made the trees and then the animals. He took some mud, and of this made first a deer; after that, he made all the other animals.

Sometimes Turtle would say, "That does not look well: can't you make it some other way?"

Some time after this, Earth-Initiate and Coyote were at Marysville Buttes. Earth-Initiate said, "I am going to make people." In the middle of the afternoon he began, for he had returned to Ta'doikö. He took dark red earth, mixed it with water, and made two figures, -one a man, and one a woman. He laid the man on his right side, and the woman on his left, inside his house. Then he lay down himself, flat on his back, with his arms stretched out. He lay thus and sweated all the afternoon and night.

Early in the morning the woman began to tickle him in the side. He kept very still, did not laugh. By and by he got up, thrust a piece of pitch-wood into the ground, and fire burst out. The two people were very white. No one to-day is as white as they were. Their eyes were pink, their hair was black, their teeth shone brightly, and they were very handsome. It is said that Earth-Initiate did not finish the hands of the people, as he did not know how it would be best to do it. Coyote saw the people, and suggested that they ought to have hands like his. Earth-Initiate said, "No, their hands shall be like mine."

Then he finished them. When Coyote asked why their hands were to be like that, Earth-Initiate answered, "So that, if they are chased by bears, they can climb trees." This first man was called Ku'ksuu; and the woman, Morning-Star Woman.

When Coyote had seen the two people, he asked Earth-Initiate how he had made them. When he was told, he thought, "That is not difficult. I'll do it myself." He did just as Earth-Initiate had told him, but could not help laughing, when, early in the morning, the woman poked him in the ribs.

As a result of his failing to keep still, the people were glass-eyed. Earth-Initiate said, "I told you not to laugh," but Coyote declared he had not. This was the first lie.

By and by there came to be a good many people. Earth-Initiate had wanted to have everything comfortable and easy for people, so that none of them should have to work.

All fruits were easy to obtain, no one was ever to get sick and die. As the people grew numerous, Earth-Initiate did not come as often as formerly, he only came to see Ku'ksuu in the night.

One night he said to him, "To-morrow morning you must go to the little lake near here. Take all the people with you. I'll make you a very old man before you get to the lake."

So, in the morning Ku'ksuu collected all the people, and went to the lake. By the time he had reached it, he was a very old man. He fell into the lake, and sank down out of sight. Pretty soon the ground began to shake, the waves overflowed the shore, and there was a great roaring under the water, like thunder. By and by Ku'ksuu came up out of the water, but young again, just like a young, man.

Then Earth-Initiate came and spoke to the people, and said, "If you do as I tell you, everything will be well. When any of you grow old, so old that you cannot walk, come to this lake, or get some one to bring you here. You must then go down into the water as you have seen Ku'ksuu do, and you will come out young again." When he had said this, he went away. He left in the night, and went up above.

All this time food had been easy to get, as Earth-Initiate had wished. The women set out baskets at night, and in the morning, they found them full of food, all ready to eat, and lukewarm. One day Coyote came along. He asked the people how they lived, and they told him that all they had to do was to eat and sleep.

Coyote replied, "That is no way to do: I can show you something better." Then he told them how he and Earth-Initiate had had a discussion before men had been made; how Earth-Initiate wanted everything easy, and that there should be no sickness or death, but how he had thought it would be better to have people work, get sick, and die.

He said, "We'll have a burning." The people did not know what he meant; but Coyote said, "I'll show you. It is better to have a burning, for then the widows can be free." So, he took all the baskets and things that the people had, hung them up on poles, made everything all ready. When all was prepared, Coyote said, "At this time you must always have games." So, he fixed the moon during which these games were to be played.

Coyote told them to start the games with a foot-race, and every one got ready to run. Ku'ksuu did not come, however. He sat in his hut alone, and was sad, for he knew what was going to occur. Just at this moment Rattlesnake came to Ku'ksuu, and said, "What shall we do now?

Everything is spoiled!" Ku'ksuu did not answer, so Rattlesnake said, "Well, I'll do what I think is best." Then he went out and along the course that the racers were to go over, and hid himself, leaving his head just sticking out of a hole.

By this time all the racers had started, and among them Coyote's son. He was Coyote's only child, and was very quick. He soon began to outstrip all the runners, and was in the lead. As he passed the spot where Rattlesnake had hidden himself, however, Rattlesnake raised his head and bit the boy in the ankle. In a minute the boy was dead.

Coyote was dancing about the home-stake. He was very happy, and was shouting at his son and praising him. When Rattlesnake bit the boy, and he fell dead, every one laughed at Coyote, and said, "Your son has fallen down, and is so ashamed that he does not dare to get up." Coyote said, "No, that is not it. He is dead."

This was the first death. The people, however, did not understand, and picked the boy up, and brought him to Coyote. Then Coyote began to cry, and every one did the same. These were the first tears. Then Coyote took his son's body and carried it to the lake of which Earth-Initiate had told them, and threw the body in. But there was no noise, and nothing happened, and the body drifted about for four days on the surface, like a log.

On the fifth day Coyote took four sacks of beads and brought them to Ku'ksuu, begging him to restore his son to life. Ku'ksuu did not answer. For five days Coyote begged, then Ku'ksuu came out of his house bringing all his bead and bear-skins, and calling to all the people to come and watch him. He laid the body on a bear-skin, dressed it, and wrapped it up carefully.

Then he dug a grave, put the body into it, and covered it up. Then he told the people, "From now on, this is what you must do. This is the way you must do till the world shall be made over."

About a year after this, in the spring, all was changed. Up to this time everybody spoke the same language. The people were having a burning; everything was ready for the next day, when in the night everybody suddenly began to speak a different language. Each man and his wife, however, spoke the same. Earth-Initiate had come in the night to Ku'ksuu, and had told him about it all, and given him instructions for the next day.

So, when morning came, Ku'ksuu called all the people together, for he was able to speak all the languages. He told them each the names of the different animals, etc., in their languages, taught them how to cook and to hunt ' gave them all their laws, and set the time for all their dances and festivals.

Then he called each tribe by name, and sent them off in different directions, telling them where they were to live. He sent the warriors to the north, the singers to the west, the flute-players to the east, and the dancers to the south. So, all the people went away, and left Ku'ksuu and his, wife alone at Ta'doikö.

By and by his wife went away, leaving in the night, and going first to Marysville Buttes. Ku'ksuu staid a little while longer, and then he also left. He too went to the Buttes, went into the spirit house, and sat down on the south side. He found Coyote's son there, sitting on the north side. The door was on the west. Coyote had been trying to find out where Ku'ksuu had gone, and where his own son had gone, and at last found the tracks, and followed them to the spirit house.

Here he saw Ku'ksuu and his son, the latter eating spirit food. Coyote wanted to go in, but Ku'ksuu said, "No, wait there. You have just what you wanted; it is your own fault. Every man will now have all kinds of troubles and accidents, will have to work to get his food, and will die and be buried. This must go on till the time is out, and Earth-Initiate comes again, and everything will be made over. You must go home, and tell all the people that you have seen your son, that he is not dead."

Coyote said he would go, but that he was hungry, and wanted some of the food.

Ku'ksuu replied, "You cannot eat that. Only ghosts may eat that food."

Then Coyote went away and told all the people, "I saw my son and Ku'ksuu, and he told me to kill myself."

So, he climbed up to the top of a tall tree, jumped off, and was killed. Then he went to the spirit house, thinking he could now have some of the food; but there was no one there, nothing at all, and so he went out, and walked away to the west, and was never seen again.

Ku'ksuu and Coyote's son, however, had gone up above.

Coyote Kills the Prairie Dogs

Coyote tied the long hair from a buffalo's leg to a stick making it look like a scalp and started off, carrying it in his hand. When he came to a prairie dog town, he told them to shut their doors and come and dance. They did so. Coyote had a stone concealed in his hand with which he hit the prairie dogs, killing them as they danced round in a circle. He told them that it was the dancing that killed them and that toward evening they would get up again. The smallest of the prairie dogs who was being carried on his mother's back called out, "He has a stone in his hand." At this, all the prairie dogs ran toward their houses which, being closed, they were unable to enter. Coyote striking at them on both sides had killed a good many.

Then Coyote brought them all together and built a large fire. When it had burned down, he separated the ashes and put in the prairie dogs to cook, putting the smallest one across the others at the top. Having arranged them, he covered them with ashes and built a fire on top. While they were cooking, he went to sleep. Wildcat, coming along, took all the prairie dogs out. He removed their tails, putting them back in the ashes, and replaced the little one on top. He carried all the remainder away with him and commenced to eat them.

When Coyote woke up, he took a stick and poked out one of the prairie dogs. Seeing that it was small he said, "O, I do not need this one," and threw it away. It fell into the top of a tree which stood close to a stream of water. Coyote then seized a tail and pulled it out. "O, the tail has burned off." He then poked around with a stick in vain. There were none.

He went to find the one he had thrown away. Seeing it lying, as he supposed in the water, he dived and searched for it in vain. When he came out of the water, he saw it still lying there. He did this four times and then lay down by the edge of the water to rest. On looking up he saw it in a tree above him. Jumping up, he got it and chewed it up bones and all.

Coyote Steals Sun's Tobacco

(Jicarilla Apache)
Based on a tale reported by
Grenville Goodwin in 1939

One day Slim Coyote started out to Sun's house.

When he got there, Sun was not home, but his wife was. "Where is my cousin Sun?" he asked.

Sun's wife said that he had gone out and was not home yet.

Coyote saw Sun's tobacco bag hanging up on the side of the house. "I came to smoke and talk with my cousin," said Slim Coyote, "so give me a smoke while I'm waiting.

He won't mind, he's my cousin." Coyote was talking to Sun's wife as if she were his mother-in-law.

She handed him the tobacco bag, and he used it to fill his own little buckskin bag. Then he quickly hid his bag and rolled a cigarette, so that he actually got off with a lot of Sun's tobacco, without her noticing. "Since my cousin hasn't come back yet, I guess I won't wait after all," Coyote told her, and started home.

Pretty soon Sun arrived. "Who's been here and gone again?" he asked, looking at his depleted tobacco bag.

"Somebody who said he was your cousin," answered his wife. She told him what had happened, and Sun was very angry.

"I'll get that fellow," he said. He went out front where he had Black Wind Horse tied, and saddled him up and set off after Coyote. Black Wind Horse could fly, and when he traveled, he made a noise like lightening.

A light rain started to fall and covered up Coyote's tracks, but Sun could still follow the thief by the ashes from his cigarette.

It kept raining, and pretty soon the tobacco Coyote had with him started to grow. Soon it was putting out leaves then flowers. At last, it ripened and dried, and the wind scattered the seeds everywhere.

When the Sun saw this, he gave up chasing Coyote and went home.

When Coyote got back to the Apache camp where he was living, he kept his tobacco for himself and wouldn't give any away.

The Apache held a council on how to get Coyote's tobacco away from him, and they decided to pretend to give him a wife.

"We're going to give you a wife," they told him.

Coyote said, "You're trying to fool me."

"No, we're not," they said, "we're really going to give you a wife."

They set up a new wickiup for Coyote, dressed a young boy as a girl, and told the boy not to let Coyote touch him until just before dawn. They made a bed in the new wickiup, and

Coyote felt so good that he gave them all his tobacco.

Just about dusk the boy dressed as a girl went over and sat down beside Coyote in his new wickiup. Slim Coyote was so excited he could not stand up but just crawled around on the ground. "Why don't you come to bed?" he said to his bride. "Let's hurry and go to bed." But the boy just sat there.

After a while, when Coyote was more and more impatient, the boy lay down by him but not close to him. "I want you to lie close," Coyote said, and tried to touch the boy.

But the boy said, "Don't!" and pushed Coyote's hand away. This kept up all night, until just before dawn Coyote made a grab and caught hold of the boy's penis. He let go right away and jumped back.

"Get away from me, get back from me; you're a boy not a girl," he said. Then Coyote got up and called the people. "You lied to me," he said. "You didn't give me a wife at all. Give me my tobacco back!"

But no matter how loudly he yelled, they wouldn't do it. This is the way the people first got tobacco.

The Maiden Who Became a Bear

(Navaho)
The Dîné: Origin Myths of the Navaho Indians Aileen O'Bryan

When the brothers returned that night, they entered the house. Not seeing the Coyote among them, their sister went out to look for him; not finding him she asked her eldest brother what they had done with her husband. The eldest brother said: "We sent him back with the meat a long time ago. We thought that you would have the meat cooked for us by now." The woman looked straight at her brothers and told them that they had killed the Coyote. The brothers said: "No, sister, we have told you the truth. We sent him back with the meat early in the day." But she accused them four times of killing her husband. Four times they gave the same answer. Then she went to the rainbow path and there she found the meat. From there she tracked the Coyote to the canyon's edge and she found where he had been killed by the Swallow People.

After the woman left her brothers to go look for the Coyote the eldest brother said: "Listen now to my words: our sister is about to do something still more evil."

When the woman returned to the house, she told her brothers that the people in the canyon had killed her husband. She would not sit down in the home. She prepared herself to go against the cliff people. First, she took her sewing awls and sharpened them; then she hid her heart and lungs as the Coyote had taught her, and turned herself into a great bear with sharp teeth and claws, and she went forth against the people of the canyon. When she came among them, they shot at her with their arrows, but they did not harm her. When she returned home, she turned back into her woman form. But every night she went out in her bear form and killed the cliff people with her teeth and claws; however, she did not eat them as a wolf or bear would have done.

It was then that the people moved into the caves in the cliff walls. The Rainbow's strength was their strength. The people, in those days, used a rainbow for their ladder as well as for their bridge. They used it and it was not difficult for them to carry up their goods and to build houses in the caves. For a long time, the people abandoned their homes on the floor of the canyon; but the bear woman followed them. She would dig up through the earth and kill them. After that they built their homes of rock in the caves.

Always when she returned to her brothers, she was in her woman form. But her name was now Esdza'shash nadle, the Woman who Became a Bear.

Soon she went out even during the day to kill people. She became so terrible that the Spider People, the Lizard People, and the Swallow People built high in the sides of the canyons where she could not reach them. After a time, the brothers became frightened. They did not know what to do. But they knew that their turn would come; that she would kill them too. The eldest brother had a plan. He, together with the other brothers, pushed the ashes of the fire to one side and they dug a hole under the fireplace. They hid the youngest brother in this hole which had four sides to hold back the earth. They covered the hole with a slab over which they put earth; they then raked the ashes over it and built a fire. Then they went to the east of their dwelling.

When the Bear Woman returned no one was in the house. She went to relieve herself and said: "Whichever way the water runs, that is the direction my brothers have taken." It showed east; so, she followed in her bear form. She tracked them and she killed the 11 brothers. She saw that the youngest was missing. She returned to the house. Again, she went to relieve herself, and she said: "Whichever way it flows there my brother is." But it neither flowed nor fell. So, she went into the house and tore the rocks out. She found her youngest brother under the firestone.

The Bear Woman spoke kind words to him. "Come out, my brother," she said, "your hair looks dirty; it needs washing and dressing; let me care for it." The little breeze whispered in the boy's ear: "She has killed your 11 brothers, and now she wants your life." The little breeze stayed on the boy's ear and told him to have weapons ready when she began to comb his hair. It told him also, to loosen the string ties of his loin cloth. "She will place you facing the sun when she starts to comb your hair; but you must sit so that. you can see her shadow." The woman made her brother sit facing the sun; but be said: "Sister, the sun is too bright for my eyes." After four times she agreed to let him sit where he chose. He sat where he could watch her shadow. She got the grass brush, which they used for the hair, and she brushed his hair once or twice; and out grew her lips to the shape of a bear's mouth with long teeth. The boy turned and said: "What is it, sister?" She said: "Oh, I am just sleepy." The breeze was now busy in the boy's ear telling him what would happen and what he should do. He was to be saved; but the price paid was the lives of his 11 brothers.

The boy was told that the fourth time that he caught her changing into the form of a bear he must jump up and run as fast as he could to the place where she had hidden her heart and lungs. "About the moment when she is about to catch you, you will jump over a big cactus. She will have to go around it and you will gain ground. The second time you will jump over a big growth of yucca; the third time, over a log; and the fourth time you will jump over a big boulder."

Now the boy watched her shadow, and each time that he caught her changing into the bear form he turned and looked at her and she became the woman. After the fourth time he had his muscles set, and jumped away from her. Sure enough, she grabbed his belt; but the tie loosened. She was near him when he reached the cactus. He jumped over it; she ran around it. The second time she was near him he jumped over the yucca; the third time he jumped over the fallen log; and the fourth time, over the great boulder. Then her heart became nervous, and the chipmunk who was guarding it screamed. The heart and the lungs were beating up and down just ahead of the boy. They were covered with oak leaves. The Bear Woman cried out: "Oh, brother, brother, stop! There are my heart and my lungs. There is my life."

Now when the boy saw the leaves beating up and down in fright, he jumped over them, and he shot his arrow into them. The Bear Woman fell, and the blood gushed out of her mouth and nostrils. The boy returned near her, and the little breeze told him to stop the blood. It must not flow, for if it met the blood from her heart, she would become whole again. So, the boy pulled the Bear Woman's carcass away. He was angry. He spread her legs and cut out her sex organs. He said: "You have the sex organs of a woman, and great trouble has come of it." He tossed it to the top of a tree and said: "The people of the earth shall use you henceforth." It became the pitch that is found on cedar and pinon trees. Then he cut off her breasts and said: "You have a woman's breasts and still you have caused great trouble."

He tossed them to the top of a tree and said: "The people of the earth shall use you." And they became pinon nuts.

After these things happened many people planned to leave the mesas. They were afraid of the Woman who became a bear. They buried the Calendar Stone; they wrapped their dead; and leaving their belongings, they went away. But before they left, they drew pictures on the rocks of all the things that trouble came from.

Now only the Swallow People and the Lizard, Snake, and Spider People remained. All the others said that they would never return to make the mesa country their home. They moved into Montezuma Valley and built their homes around Ute Mountain. Their main dwellings were Yucca House and a place near a spring east of Ute Mountain. They multiplied and their homes covered quite a lot of territory. They moved to places where they found good water, good building material, and where their plants would grow. But always they came to where their chief person lived. This was a place west of Dolores called Sage Brush Spring. They moved their chief, or head person of their tribe, there. This person was considered sacred, and kept away from the sun and the light all of the time. Where he lived sacred stones were placed at his feet, at his out-stretched arms and head. Prayer sticks guarded his body. Then bluebird feathers were set around him. Whatever he said was done. They lived for a time at Sage Brush Spring; but corn did not grow well there; living was difficult. They moved to the foot of Elk Mountain.

Creation and Longevity

(Achomawi)
Myths and Legends of California and the Old Southwest, by Katharine Berry Judson, 1912

Coyote began the creation of the earth, but Eagle completed it.
Coyote scratched it up with his paws out of nothingness, but Eagle complained there were no mountains for him to perch on.

So, Coyote made hills, but they were not high enough. Therefore, Eagle scratched up great ridges. When Eagle flew over them, his feathers dropped down, took root, and became trees. The pin feathers became bushes and plants.

Coyote and Fox together created man. They quarreled as to whether they should let men live always or not.

Coyote said, "If they want to die, let them die."

Fox said, "If they want to come back, let them come back."

But Coyote's medicine was stronger, and nobody ever came back. Coyote also brought fire into the world, for the Indians were freezing. He journeyed far to the west, to a place where there was fire, stole some of it, and brought it home in his ears.

He kindled a fire in the mountains, and the Indians saw the smoke of it, and went up and got fire.

The Coyote and the Balolookong

(Water Serpent)
(Oraibi)
Told by
Puhu'nomtiwa

Aliksai! The Oraibis were living in their village. There were many of them. The Balolookong was living at Flute Spring (Lanangva), west of the village. Somewhat south of this spring, at Ishmovala, the Coyote was living. They were great friends and often visited each other. One time Balolookong came out of his kiva in the spring and went over to his friend's kiva, which he entered, filling it up entirely so that the Coyote had to go out and remain there while they were conversing. After they had conversed a while, Balolookong returned to his kiva.

The Coyote was angry that he had to remain outside and was meditating how he could take revenge on his friend, and finally formed a plan. He went to the woods and brought with him a large armful of cedar bark and also some yucca leaves. He wrapped the bark with leaves, always adding wool to it so that it finally formed a large artificial tail. This he tied to his own tail and then went over to pay his friend a visit. Entering the kiva of the latter, he also kept going around until his tail filled the entire kiva, and Balolookong had to go out and also remain outside while they conversed with each other.

When they were through talking, the Coyote left, and had not yet quite left the kiva when Balolookong rushed into the kiva and shoved the artificial tail of the Coyote on the fireplace and set it on fire. When the Coyote had drawn it out of the kiva entirely, the grass through which he was running was set on fire. He thought that the people of the village were trying to drive him away by setting the grass on fire, and so he ran westward, setting everything on fire that he came in contact with. Finally, he reached the Little Colorado River. By this time the fire on his tail had reached his natural tail and he jumped into the river and tried to swim across, but perished.

Balolookongwuu and the Coyote

(Shupaulavi)
Told by Sik'ahpiki

Aliksai! In Mishongnovi, where there are now the ruins of old Mishongnovi, they were living. East of there the Lolo'okong also lived, and south from there, at Jack-Rabbit House (Coviihkivee), lived the Coyote. He was a friend of the Lolo'okong. "I am going to visit my friend," the Lolo'okong said one day, so in the evening he went over to his friend's kiva. The Lolo'okong was very long. When he arrived at the Coyote's house the latter said, "Come in." "All right," he replied. "Come in," his friend repeated, so he went in and kept coiling up until he filled the entire kiva. So, they were sitting and conversing there. "Now let us eat something," the Coyote said. "Very well," his visitor replied. So, the Coyote brought forth some juniper berries, which they ate. "Thanks, that I have eaten," the Lolo'okong said.

By this time, it had become quite late. "I am going home now," the Lolo'okong said. "All right," his host replied, "it is getting late." And after having invited the Coyote to visit him also, the Lolo'okong left. After his visitor had left the Coyote was thinking: "What shall I do to my friend, as I want to repay him?" The next day he went into the timber and got a big armful of dry cedar bark. This he tied into a long rope, as it were, with yucca leaves, and rolled it up in his kiva. He then fastened it to his tail and went out. After having run around for some time, he went to his friend's house. "Have you come?" the latter said. "Yes, I have come." "All right, come in, come in," the Lolo'okong said. So, he went in and kept circling around and around and around, filling the whole kiva with his long tail. On the walls of the kiva of the Lolo'okong were hanging many snake costumes, and the Coyote kept looking and looking at them. "Now let us eat," the host finally said, and getting from a shelf a very small bowl with some corn-pollen, set it before his visitor. "This I am eating; eat of it too," he said to the Coyote. So, they talked together until evening. "It is evening," finally the Coyote said. "I am going home now." "Very well," the Lolo'okong replied, "we are through talking, and it is evening."

The Coyote hereupon left the kiva, dragging his long tail after him. When the latter was nearly unwound, the Lolo'okong put a little piece of ember on the tail, which set it on fire, a lid when this was dragged out of the kiva, it set the grass on fire. The Coyote looked around and was wondering who was setting everything on fire after him. When the tail was nearly consumed, he had arrived at his kiva, and then he began to think that maybe his friend had done that to him. "Well now," he said, "he is my friend, and that friend has treated me this way," And then he became very angry at the Lolo'okong. He then entered his kiva and continued to live there.

The Coyote and the Frog

Aliksai! Along time ago the people were living in Walpi. North of the village lived the Coyote. In the spring called Sun Spring (Tawaba) lived the Frog. They were friends with each other.

So, one time the Coyote went over to visit his friend, the Frog. He ascended the mesa and passed by the village. The dogs of the village, noticing him, made a raid on him, He ran and jumped down the mesa, but was not killed.

Arriving at his friend, the Frog, he first drank a great deal of water. "Thanks that I have had this drink," he said to the Frog. "I was very thirsty." "Now, let us sit down," the Frog said. ,'You sit down there at the edge of the water and dance for me," the Coyote said to the Frog.

So, the Frog jumped down into the deep water from where he was sitting and passed down to the bottom, but immediately came up again having his mouth wide open. He was pregnant. "Draw me out," he said to the Coyote, so the Coyote grasped him by the arms and forcibly threw him onto the ground close to the water. Hereupon the Frog burst and it was found that he was full of little tadpoles which were swarming around him. But the Frog himself died.

"Oh!" the Coyote said, "why did you jump into that water there. I shall run home now."

So, he started off, went up the mesa and by Sitcomovi. When the children of Sitcomovi saw him, they said: "There a Coyote is running." The people living in Hano now also noticed him. "There is a Coyote! There is a Coyote! There is a Coyote!" they said, whereupon they followed him, trying to capture him.

By this time a heavy rain and hail storm came up. The Coyote ran for his hole, but found that it had been filled up with water so that he could not get in. Heavy hail stones were by this time falling upon him and he was running around trying to find some shelter, but the hail stones were so heavy that he was finally killed by them.

The Coyote, the Bat, and the Hummingbird

(Shupaulavi) (Oraibi)
Told by Kuhkiuma
(Shupaulavi) And
Qoyawaima (Oraibi)

A long time ago the Coyote lived at Ishmovala, west of the village; a Bat at Tovitoala, north-west of the village; and a Humming-bird at Tohchipchookpu, also north-west of the village. They were all three close friends.

The Bat and the bird often visited the Coyote, spending their time there in joking, laughing, and eating. The Coyote, being a great hunter, always had plenty of rabbit meat and other game, which he would cook and place before them, and which they enjoyed very much.

One time the Bat thought that he would invite his two friends to his house, but he was worried as to what he would give them to eat, so his thoughts were directed to the village of Oraibi. He said to himself: "I am going to the village after dark and perhaps some one of the rich people may have forgotten to take their meat in that they are drying, and I am going to get some of it."

So ill the evening, he proceeded to the village and was flying around, but found no meat; so he went home discouraged. "Now what shall I do?" he thought. "I am going to try it again, and perhaps I shall find an open window through which I can get into some house and find some food inside." This he did, and finding at one place some tallow, he broke off a piece and carried it home.

Returning to the same house he got some more. Hereupon he procured some meat in the same manner, making also several trips after meat. He then in the same manner procured some piki, of which he fetched a goodly supply to his house. "Now, my friends will want some salt with this food," he thought, and so he went in search of some salt, which he found and carried to his house.

After he had thus laid in a supply of food for his anticipated visitors, he commenced to think what he should say to them when they would inquire as to the source where he obtained the food. He began thinking of some one that was his friend and whose name he could mention, and thought of the Badger, who lived east of Oraibi, at Badger-Ditch (Honancik'a). Hereupon he retired but did not sleep much that night, as he was very busy thinking over the anticipated visit of his two friends.

In the morning he proceeded to the house of the Coyote, and from there to that of the Hummingbird, inviting them to visit him that day. They promptly accepted the invitation and paid their friend a visit. At noon the Bat said, "Now let us eat." Whereupon he prepared a meal of the things he had procured.

First, he fried some of the meat, which he then placed in a bowl in which he had melted some of the tallow. They then ate, enjoying the food very much. While they were eating, they were wondering where their friend procured the food, and in the course of their conversation, which was very animated, they asked him about it. He promptly stated that his friend, the Badger, had given it to him.

They doubted it, said nothing, but when they went home, soon after the meal, they talked about the matter and agreed that their friend had probably deceived them. Before they parted, the Coyote invited the bird to visit him in the evening. This the bird did, and their conversation soon again turned upon the subject of the food which they had so much enjoyed at their friend's house. They again were wondering where he procured it, but soon agreed that he must have stolen it in Oraibi, and that he had deceived them,

1n order to get even with their friend, they concluded that they would "song-tie" him, that is, they would make a song about their friend. They at once started to compose a song, but did not finish it to their satisfaction.

So, after the Humming-bird had left, the Coyote kept thinking over the song, and during the night, while he could not sleep, finished it. The next morning, he at once went to the house of the bird, to whom he sang this song, to the satisfaction of both of them:

Sawya, Sawya!
Bat, Bat!
Tucivakiota, tucivakiota.
In the hollow, In the hollow!
Anawit kwitaat
Along its excrements
Tucanmuruta, tucanmuruta
A ridge (of) dirt, a ridge (of) dirt!
Kikanqo, kikanqo
To the village, to the village.

The following is supposed to be the complaint of the party whose food the bat carried off:

Iyumukvi, akwihkwistkae
From my inner chamber, because fat he got
Kalatoto matototimaia.
The Kalatoto are running about.

They practiced the song until they both knew it. Hereupon the Coyote returned to his house, the Humming-bird saying he would invite the Bat to come over in the evening, which he did. When the Bat arrived, the bird went over to the Coyote's house, telling him that their friend was waiting for them. The Coyote at once also proceeded to the house of the bird, where the latter soon proposed to have a song. The Bat consented, saying that they wanted to be happy together.

So, they stood up in a line and the bird commenced to sing the song which the Coyote had made. The Coyote at once chimed in and the Bat also commenced to sing with them the best he could, but soon found out that a joke was being played on him, and that he was being song-tied by his two friends.

As soon as he had found this out, he stopped singing and became angry. "You have song-tied me," he said to the others. "The Coyote has made the song; you both have made it. Now this ends our friendship." Whereupon they dispersed and never became friends again.

How the Coyote Was Deceived by the Wren
(Oraibi)
Told by Tangakhoyoma

Haliksai! A long time ago, when they were living in Oraibi, the Coyote Woman lived at Ishmovala. She had four children. She always went hunting mice and other little animals, which she brought to her children and fed them to the latter. She went to the spring, Flute Spring (La'nva) and Dawn Spring (Talaova), after water for her children, but as she had no water vessel, she brought the water in her mouth. When she had given one of the children to drink, she would run again and get some more for the other children until they were all satisfied. In that way she was feeding and watering her children.

One time she again went after water to the Dawn Spring, filling her mouth very full. When she returned, she saw a Wren sitting on a rock, and when she came near the bird, the latter was jumping up and down from one rock to another singing as follows:

Calapongki, cholo, cholo,
Calapongki, cholo, cholo,
Riuw, riuw.

When the Coyote saw it, she had to laugh, and spilled the water from her mouth. "Now then, why are you dancing there that way that I had to laugh and spill my water; I shall have to get some more," whereupon she ran back to the spring to get some more water. When she came back with her mouth full, she thought that this time she was not going to laugh, but when she arrived at the place where the Tu'chvo was dancing and saw the latter dance and heard him singing in the same manner, she again had to laugh, saying: "Poah," by which she again spilled the water. But this time she was angry and said: "Why are you dancing and singing here that way that I have to spill this water? My children are thirsty and they will die. Now, I am going back to get some more water, and if you are doing that still when I return and I spill the water again, I shall devour you." Hereupon she returned to the spring to fill her mouth again.

While the Coyote was gone the Wren slipped out of its skin and dressed up a stone with the skin so that it looked like a Wren. This artificial bird he put up where he had been sitting and he himself slipped under a rock, waiting for the Coyote. When the latter came along the Wren began singing the same song from under the rock. The Coyote began to laugh, saying: "Poah" and spilled the water. She was now very angry. "Now then," she said, "you are still singing that way here and I am going to devour you," whereupon she grabbed the stone dressed in the bird's skin and crushed it. She broke all her teeth so that the blood was streaming from her mouth.

She ran back to the Dawn Spring in order to wash her face, but as she stooped over the water, she saw some on-e with a bloody face staring at her. She at once left the spring without having drunk any water, and ran to Spider Spring, where she was scared away in the same manner. From here she ran to Dripping Spring (Shivukva), where she met with the same disappointment. Hereupon she ran to Hotval Spring (Hotvalva). Here again she was scared away by the face staring at her, and without daring to drink she rushed away westward to the Grand Canyon. Arriving at the rim of the Canyon she jumped into the canyon and perished.

The Aahtu and the Coyote

(Oraibi)
Told by Qoyawaima

A long time ago many Aahtu were playing in the cedar timber north of Oraibi. One time they were near a very pretty cedar-tree and here they sang the following song:

Hatava, yayhona yuhina,
Hatava yayhona,
Hatava yayhona,
Tuva yayhona!

The meaning of the words is not known, except "tu'va" (throw). "Hatava" may be an obsolete word for "eyes."

When they were through with the song, they all took out their eyes, throwing them on the tree, where they remained suspended like little balls. They then sang the same song again, whereupon the eyes returned to their sockets. This they did many times. All at once a Coyote appeared upon the scene and asked: "What are you doing here?" "Yes," they said, "we are having a little dance here, and then we play throwing our eyes on the tree and getting them back again. Sometimes when the eyes are not very clear and one throws them away in this manner, they become clear again." "All right," the Coyote said, "I shall join you because one of my eyes is not very clear. Some time ago I was chasing a rabbit and ran with my head against a tree and a piece of wood entered my eye, and ever since that eye is very dim, so I shall play with you and maybe my eye will get clear."

So, they sang their little song again, the Coyote joining them, and as they sang the last word, they all threw their eyes on the tree, the Coyote too. They then sang again, and all the eyes, except those of the Coyote, returned. The little Birds all laughed at him saying, "Your eyes will never return; you are bad (unaihu), you are taking other people's things away sometimes, and that is the reason why your eye got hurt with that stick; your eyes will never come back; you are dangerous; and you are going to die somewhere." The Coyote was very angry and left them. As he could not find anything to eat now, he soon died. The place where he died was called Coyote-Death-Place (ishmo'mokpu) ever since.

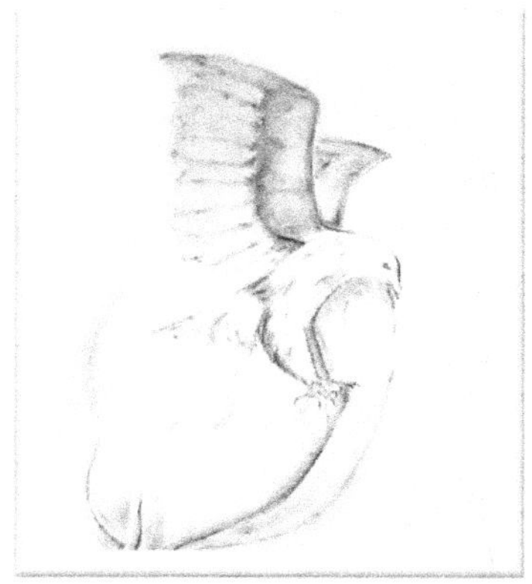

The Coyote and the Red Eagle

(Shupaulavi)
Told by Sik'ahpik'i
(Shupaulavi) and
Lomavantiwa (Shupaulavi)

In Mishongnovi the people were living. North of the village at the bluff Kwana Vuvi lived the Red Eagle, and east of the village at Where-Coyotes'-Heads-are-put-in (Ishqottangat), lived the Coyote. He had children. During the day it was very hot and he went to hunt something for them, but did not kill anything. So, he returned to his children, who were very thirsty. They were living only a very short time. Now he went after water for them to Toriva, but he had no jug, so he got water in his mouth. When he arrived there, he drank and drew out his mouth full of water. With his mouth full of water, he ran to his children and now he arrived at Kwanavuvi, and there on the bluff sat the Red Eagle. He danced on one leg and sang as follows:

Tipoki homponcholo
Yep nu (Here I)
Cholo, cholo, chololololo.

The Coyote laughed at the Red Eagle and spilled the water. Now he ran back to the spring again, and again filled his mouth with water. Now he ran again, and again arrived at the Red Eagle, who was still dancing, and because he (the Coyote) laughed again, he again poured out the water. Now the Coyote was angry. "Why do you dance here that way?" he asked the Red Eagle. "Now let me go to the cedar timber and hunt some pitch," and he ran very fast to the timber, and there a pinon-tree had a great deal of pitch. He cut that off and carrying it, went home. Now he again descended to Toriva and drank there, very much, because he was very thirsty. When he had drank, he filled his mouth and then pasted up his mouth with the pitch.

Now he again came to the Red Eagle, who was again dancing. The Coyote again laughed, but his mouth was closed up tightly and he did not spill the water. Now at last he ran to his children very fast. When he arrived there, they were sleeping nicely. When he had taken off the pitch he poured the water into their mouths, but they did not get awake. Why, they had died! Now because he was very angry, he wanted to kill the Red Eagle, and went to him, very angry. When he arrived there the Red Eagle flew away. When he flew away, he showed him his leg and, behold! he had two legs. The Coyote jumped at him but did not catch him, and thus he did not kill him.

The Badger and the Coyote

(Shupaulavi)
Told by Sik'ahpik'i

Haliksai! North-east of Walpi at Oaktoika lived the Coyote. West of this place at Shiwapba lived the Badger. They were friends. One time the latter visited his friend, the Coyote. "Have you come?" the Coyote said. "Yes," his friend replied. Hereupon they conversed until noon. "Now let us have something to eat," the Coyote said, whereupon he went into a room and got out some juniper berries. "This I am eating," he said to his friend, and set it before him. "Now, eat this," he said. Hereupon they ate. When that was eaten, they conversed until towards evening, when the Badger said he had to go home now. "Very well," the Coyote replied. And after having invited his friend to visit him too, the Badger went home. In the evening he went on a hunt and tracking a rabbit into a hole he quickly dug him up and pulled him out. Having killed the rabbit, he took him home and put him away until the next morning.

Early in the morning he roasted the rabbit nicely and then waited for his friend, who soon came. "Have you come?" the Badger said. "Yes," the Coyote said. "Very well," the Badger said. So, they conversed all forenoon and at noon the Badger said: "Now, we are going to have something to eat, too," whereupon he brought forth the roasted rabbit, which looked very inviting. Cutting the rabbit up, the Badger invited his friend to eat, whereupon they enjoyed their meal very much. When they had eaten, they again conversed with each other, and were very happy talking about the good food that they had eaten. Towards evening the Coyote said that he must go home now. "Very well," the Badger replied, whereupon the Coyote left, his friend having wished him a happy journey. After that each one continued to live in his house.

The Badger, the Coyote, and the Kohonino Maiden

(Oraibi)
Told by Lomanomtiwa

Haliksai! In Oraibi the people were living. At Badger Gulch (Honancika), lived the Badger. His friend the Coyote lived at Ishmovala. The two were great friends. One time they were hunting together. They were hunting and had gotten as far as Mowahpi, quite a distance west of Apohnivi, but they had not killed anything. Some time before the Coyote had been hunting alone and had found the place where a Kohonino maiden had died some time previously. So, he said to his friend the Badger: "Let us go and hunt the place where the Kohonino maiden has died, and let us revive her. You are a doctor and will certainly know how to do it." So, they went to the place and there sure enough found the bones.

They gathered the bones and placed them on a pile. The Badger had on a black kilt (kokomvitkuna). This he spread over the bones. The Coyote was anxious to see what his friend would do, but his friend said he should not stay there, but he should go away, he should hide somewhere. Then the Badger was thinking that the maiden would have to have some flesh and some color, so he sent the Coyote westward to Coho'h-toika to get some dry grass. When the Coyote brought this, they put some of the grass with the bones. He then sent the Coyote to a place west of Mowahpi

112

to get some red paint (cuta). Of this he also put a small quantity under the black kilt, He then sent the Coyote to a spring called Hidden Spring (Nauyva), to get some water from there. When he returned, they poured a little of the water in a bowl and wet the paint with it.

The Badger now told the Coyote to go away. He went away but soon sneaked back again, crawling towards the place where his friend was working over the bones. The Badger was angry and said to him that if he did not go away, and if he saw that, the maiden would never revive. Hereupon he drove the Coyote off, and the latter went away quite a distance this time. Then the Badger sang as follows:

Hatataplocho, lochoooo,
Hatataplocho, lochoooo,
Payapim, Kohninapim,
Nowacha' pim waya! waya!
Momoka, momoka ai, ai.

Hereupon he poured some of the paint over the bones and grass. He then repeated the song several times, always pouring some of the paint over the material as he concluded the song. All at once the bones began to move under the cover. He waited a little and then removed the cover and, behold I the maiden was alive. She sat up and looked around. "Why do you want me?" she asked. "It is not I that wanted you," he said, "but the Coyote," whereupon he called the latter. The Coyote came running and the Badger said to him: "You wanted me to revive this one, now she is alive again," "Yes," he said, "it was I who wanted it that way." This way they talked together and then they said they wanted to go home, and told the maiden so. She was willing to go with them.
As they went home the Coyote coveted the mana and wanted to marry her, but the Badger was not willing. He

said: "That is not the purpose for which we brought her to life. She was to be our clan sister (tu'mci). We wanted her to build the fire for us." They finally came to Big Hill (Wopachomo), and the Coyote was anxious to have the maiden. He rushed upon her and bit her in the calf of her leg. The Badger was very angry, saying: "Why did you do that? That is not the reason why we brought her. You are bad." As he was saying this the maiden fell down and died again.

They were thinking where they should bury her. So, the Badger took the body on his back and took it south-west. The Coyote followed him a short distance then returned to the place where she had died, but he soon again followed, overtaking the Badger. "Why did you follow me?" asked the Badger. "One does not follow the dead." In a little while the Coyote again ran back to the place where the maiden had died. "When he comes back again," the Badger said to himself: "I shall not say anything to him. But how shall I kill him? He is bad." In a little while he put down the corpse and began to dig a grave. As he was working at it the Coyote returned. So, they here buried the maiden and then returned home.

But it was evening when they came to the Coyote's house. Here they both remained over night. In the morning the Badger went to his home, inviting his friend, however, to come and visit him the next day. As he went home, he was thinking how he should kill the Coyote. As he went along, he killed some bull-snakes (lolo'okongs). When he arrived at his home, he had killed four of them. On his fireplace was standing a pot. He cut the lolo'okongs up into short pieces and put the pieces into the drying pot. He stirred then, over a slow fire until they were thoroughly dry. The lolo'okongs were fat. When he was done with this he put on another pot and made some hurushuki. As he was done with that his friend came.

"My friend," the Coyote said. "Ha!" the Badger replied. "Are you in?" the Coyote asked. "Yes," he said, "come in, come in." So, the Coyote went in and they commenced to eat right away. When they were through eating the Coyote asked the Badger: "What have you here that tasted so good?" "Yes," said the Badger, who had a knife in his hand. "I did not know what to set before you, and so I cut open my abdomen, took my entrails out and roasted them for you, and before I was through, my abdomen was closed up again." The Coyote would not believe him. "Certainly, you did not roast that, yet you are saying it," the Coyote said. "Yes," the Badger replied, "I roasted that. You see my abdomen is not quite well yet," whereupon he showed it to him, having made a little scratch on it beforehand. And then the Coyote believed him. "I am going to do that, too," the Coyote said. "You come and visit me tomorrow morning. But I have no knife and roasting pot; you have a knife and a pot, let me have them." "Very well," the Badger said, you take them along." He gave him the knife and the pot, and then the Coyote left the kiva and ran home. After he had left the Badger said: "Get out, old man, you will certainly die, believing me that way."

When the Coyote got home, he went to sleep. In the morning he put the pot on the fire and then leaned against the wall. He took the knife and opened his abdomen a little, but it hurt him, and he turned away. "Oh my! I shall not die," he thought, and then made a larger cut. He then laid down the knife and took hold of the edge with his four paws and tore a big opening in his abdomen, whereupon the entrails dropped out. He moaned very much when he opened his abdomen, saving "Ana-na-na-na-na-na-." He then took hold of one of the larger intestines and thereupon fell over and died.

When the Badger came over, he looked in and said, "Friend (Kwach)," but receiving no answer he entered. He found that his friend was dead. He said: "Of course, you died here, being deceived that way. Of course, I did not really open my abdomen. You have been deceived." Hereupon he took the fat from the Coyote, and returned to his house. Close to his house was an ant hill. He spread this fat over the ant hill, whereupon the ants moved away, and that is the reason why the ants do not remain when coyote fat is placed where they are, and that is also the reason why coyote fat is used for ant bites.

The Coyote and the Kokontu Maidens

(Oraibi)
Told by Kwayeshva

Haliksai! At Munaovi the Kokontu (Sing Kona) were living. But they were all maidens and were constantly grinding corn. There was a long row of them, and they were singing as they ground the corn. One time the Coyote came around and was going up and down there. "There," he said, "there is somebody here singing." So, he went up and saw a number of maidens grinding corn. When he came to the house, he looked through the window where they were grinding corn. They sang the following song:

Talaw no'nonga, early we go out,

Nononga, ma! We go out, see!
(Referring to the custom of going out early in the. morning [kuivato] and sprinkling meal towards the east.)

The Coyote listened to them and looked at them. By this time the Kokontu noticed the Coyote. "Come in" they said to him" How I shall get in, you have such a small house," he said. "All right, you talk to us from outside," they said. And then they said to one another: "Let us go out and do something." So, they came out and went to a steep bluff south of where they lived, where there was a large pinon-tree growing at the edge of the bluff. The Coyote went with them and here they now played, running up the tree on one side and jumping down the tree and from the bluff on some sand that had piled up at the foot of the bluff. As they could run up steep bluffs, they would repeat this constantly, jumping down, coming up again, jumping down, coming up again, and so on. The Coyote looked on and envied them because they could do this. "You are enjoying yourselves," the Coyote said to them, "I shall join you." "All right," they replied, "you come and play with us." "But when I shall jump down there, I shall hurt myself," he said. "No," they replied, "that will not hurt you at all."

Hereupon he joined them, ran and played with them, and finally climbed up the tree, too. When he saw the Kokontu constantly jump down he also jumped down, but before he had reached the bottom he was circling around in the air and landed forcibly on the ground, and of course was killed. The Kokontu laughed at him, saying: "You fool, that you did as we did. We are not heavy, and nothing happened to us, but you are too heavy for that." So, when they had laughed at him, they went home again, leaving him there dead.

The Coyote and the Grasshoppers

(Shupaulavi)
Told by Lomavantiwa

Aliksai! The people were living in Shongopavi. North of the village (about three miles), was a bluff in which a Sparrow-hawk had his house (nest). A short distance (about half a mile), north of Shongopavi was a sand hill in which lived many Grasshoppers. These the Sparrow-hawk relished very much and was constantly watching them. When he would see the little Grasshoppers jumping about, he would swoop down on them and carry them to his children, who would quickly devour them. There were ten Grasshopper children, all of whom the Sparrow-hawk killed, one after another. When they were all gone their parents mourned over the loss of their children.

At this juncture a Coyote came along, saying to the Grasshopper mother: "You are singing nicely. Sing to me, too." "No," she insisted, "I am not singing, I am crying. This Sparrow-hawk killed all my children and I am crying." But the Coyote would not listen, and said: "If you do not sing to me, I will devour you." Hereupon the Grasshopper mother repeated her song:

Wala, wala, chochon nacomta,
Tumaci kele nanakavoo
Itimuy uuyinglawu

Uy, uy, h- h- h- (with a rising inflection to represent sobbing).

The Coyote at once ran away singing the song of the Grasshopper. Arriving at a rock he stumbled over it and fell down, losing by that the song. He tried to sing it again but was just able to say the first syllable, WA, WA. So, he returned to the place where he had left the Grasshopper woman, the latter, however, had also left the place immediately after the departure of the Coyote, leaving in her place a stone that resembled the form of the Grasshopper. Arriving at this stone the Coyote said, "I have forgotten my song, sing it to me again," but received no reply. "If you do not sing, I shall devour you," he said, "but still receiving no reply he grabbed the stone and broke his teeth. The blood was running from his mouth. In this condition he ran about to hunt food, but even when he found some, he could not eat it as he had no teeth, and so finally he perished with hunger.

The Coyote and the Grasshopper

(Oraibi)
Told by Macahongva

Haliksai! In Oraibi the people were living at Grasshopper Bluff (To'tolchomo), the Grasshopper Old Man (To'tol Wuhtaka) and his wife were living. They had children. At Ishmovala lived the Coyote. It was planting time. The Grasshopper had a big field east of where he lived. The two were great friends. When it was planting time, the Grasshopper also wanted to plant but he said to his wife that he was not going to plant alone, others were going to help him, so she should put up a good deal of food. She prepared some muhpiki, some qo'ma, and filled a jug with water. All this her husband took on his back, took some seeds, and went to his field. Here he seated himself in the kisi that he had built in his field and waited, but nobody came. It was nearly noon and still nobody came. So, he ate his food all alone. When he had eaten, he took the seed, went into the field and planted all alone. In the afternoon it became very hot and he was thirsty, so he returned to the kisi, drank some water and lay down to rest, leaning his feet against the side of the booth.

While he was lying there in that manner, he heard somebody come. It was his friend the Coyote. "Well now," the latter said, "why is my friend lying down that way?" "Yes," the Grasshopper replied, "I am lying here because I am tired. I am afraid this kisi will fall down on me, and how shall I run away?" "Now, let me lie down, too," the Coyote said, so he lay down beside his friend, also leaning his hind feet against the booth. The Grasshopper jumped up then, said that his water in the jug was about gone and he would get me more water. Picking up the jug he went to his house where he found his children. As he was planning some mischief against his friend, he told his children to go before him to their uncle, the Deer, who lived at Cotton Field Mount (Pichinvaschomo).

The Coyote was, during this time, lying in the kisi with his hind legs against the timbers of the booth. He waited and waited, and finally became tired. "I guess my friend is not coming," he said, "I guess he lied and it is not true that this kisi will fall down on me. I shall at least try to let. Go with my feet and quickly jump out." So, he did so, and while the booth was shaking it did not fall. "There," he said, "he just lied to me. I shall go and eat up his children." So, he went to the house of his friend and found the door closed with a grass mat. This he removed and went in, but found no one in the house. "Aha," he said, "they have run away from me," and coming out of the house he found their tracks leading north-eastward.

He followed the tracks and came to the house of the Deer. "Has the Grasshopper come here with his family?" he asked. "Yes," the Deer replied, "they have come here." "You get them out here," the Coyote said. "No, you come in yourself, the Deer replied." No, no, bring them out," the Coyote insisted, "I want to devour them." "No, no, you come in yourself," the Deer once more said. So, the Coyote went down the ladder two rungs and then jumped out again. "Oh," he exclaimed. "Do not be afraid," the Deer said, "we are not going to hurt you." So, he again went down two rungs, but jumped out again, being afraid. "You just go in," the Deer said, "we shall not hurt you." "No, you bring them out here," the Coyote once more requested. But finally, he concluded to go down. He stopped at the elevated portion of the kiva, and saw two strong Deer standing one on each side of the fireplace. In another part of the kiva, he saw the wife of the Grasshopper and her children. "You hand those to me here," he said to the Deer. "No, you come down yourself, and get them," they replied. So, he stepped down into the deeper portion of the kiva, but at once one of the Deer picked him up with the horns and threw him upward towards the hatchway. As soon as he fell down the other Deer picked him up and threw him upwards, and so they kept it up until he was dead, whereupon they threw him out.

Hereupon the Deer said to the Grasshoppers: "Now, you go out wherever you think, nobody will hurt you now." When they had left the kiva, their mother said to them: "Now, every one of you go where he wants to go," so they immediately scattered, flying in all directions, and that is the reason why the grasshoppers are now found everywhere. If they had not scattered out at that time, they would be just living at one place now.

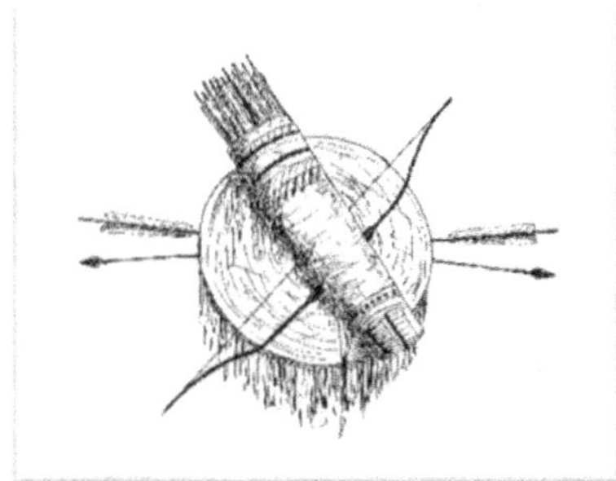

The Three Maidens and the Coyote

(Oraibi)
Told by Qoyawaima

Haliksai! In Oraibi the people were living. Over there at Howakapchomo somebody, some maidens had a crop. They had a father and a mother; three maidens there were. They were living at Pik'atsva. From there they went to watch their crop; and now at Ishmovala lived the Coyote. He had eaten watermelons, but he was longing for those maidens. Them he wanted.

The Coyote had a grandmother and to her he said: "My grandmother!" "Ha!" she said. "Shall I not start south for those maidens?" "O my!" she said, "they certainly will not want you, but if you want to go to them, you go to the village and there somewhere you enter through a window opening, and if there is a bow hanging anywhere, take it; also if there is an arrow quiver, take that, too; also red yarn, and if you find some blue yarn take that, too; also if you find some leggings, take them; and then a blue shirt; and if you go somewhere in the rear of the village and find some red stone ochre, take it. That much you come and bring." Thus, she said to him.

Now the Coyote started for the village and arrived there, and sure enough, he found a broken bow somewhere and took it. Also, an arrow quiver he found, which he also took; and a shirt, and leggings; some blue yarn, and stone ochre. That much he brought along. Now he went to his grandmother. The grandmother dressed him up in it. He put on the shirt and the leggings, had his hair tied up, put the quiver with arrows behind his loin string. Now the ochre he put on his face like the Hoha' Katcina, and thus he went to the maidens. But the father of the maidens had put up a stone trap east of the Coyote's house, and now the Coyote went to the maidens, but he arrived at that trap, and there at the balance some rabbit meat was tied. When he arrived there, he pressed towards it (the meat), but he was fooled. He went into the trap and took hold of the meat with his teeth and pulled at it, and of course, the trap shut and thus he died there.

When it was evening those maidens going home went to the trap of their father and arrived there, and there that (Coyote) was caught and they laughed at him when they saw that some one with an arrow quiver was sticking out there. When they had seen him, they went home and when they arrived there they slept during the night, but in the evening, they said to their father: "Our father," one said "Hay!" he said. "In your trap there, something has been caught." "Very well," he said, "to-morrow I shall also go there." When it had become morning, the father went there and arrived at his trap, and sure enough he (Coyote) was caught. He pulled him out and carried him to his field. When he arrived there, he skinned him and hung up his skin as a watching flag. And after that it was hanging there as a flag.

How the Coyotes Had a Katcina Dance

(Oraibi)
Told by Kwayeshva

At Squash Seed Point (Batangvoc Toika), lived the Ha'aa Katcina. North of there, lived the Hototo Katcina. At Putatokaovi lived the Soho'ncomtaka Katcina, north of the village lived the Red Eagle (Palakway) Katcina, and at Katcinvala lived many Katcinas. At Ishmovala lived the Coyote and his wife. The Coyote used to see the Katcinas come and have their dances and processions, and one time said to his wife: "We are going to do that, too. People like to see this."

In the morning the Coyote went out, and standing on the roof of his kiva he called out to his friends, the Coyotes, that they should assemble in his kiva. Soon they came from come from all sides, many of them. When they had all assembled, he said to them: "I want to 'overtake' something, too, like these Katcinas do. To-morrow we shall have a Katcina dance. So you go to the village, and if you find something in the rear of the village such as feathers, pieces of skin, etc., bring it here." They all declared themselves willing. The Coyotes thus went out and went around the village hunting for pieces of skin, feathers, pieces of gourds, especially the necks of long necked gourds, and brought all these things to the Coyote's kiva. Here they sewed up kilts, made bunches of feathers for head-dresses, etc., thus working all day. Each one prepared a costume of a Katcina that he had seen. During the night they slept there.

In the morning one of the Coyotes went to the place where the Ha'aa Katcina always dresses up; two others to the place where the Hototo dresses up: one to the place of the Soho'ncomtaka; one dressed up like the Palakwayo at the place where that Katcina lives; and a number of others went to Katcinvala. When all were ready the Ha'aa shouted four times and then went northward where he was joined by the two Hototos, then by the next ones, and these by the Palakway, and finally by the Katcinas at Katcinvala. They all then went to the Coyote's house at Ishmovala. The Coyote and his wife, who lived here had not gone along but had remained with their children. Here the Katcinas now had a dance.

The Oraibi happened to have a Coyote hunt on this day. Some of them went southward, others northward, from the village, forming a large circle, and then proceeding towards the village. But they found no Coyotes because the latter were all assembled at Ishmovala. While they were still dancing, the Oraibi came upon them and at once closed in upon them. When the Coyotes saw that they were surrounded they began to run, trying to escape, but as they had masks on, they could not see so well, and many of them were killed at once; others threw down their masks, but as they had their Costumes on, they could not run fast and so were also killed. Only the family that lived at Ishmovala, and who had not put on costumes or masks, escaped. When the Hopi had killed all the Coyotes, they laughed at them and went to the village, being happy over their successful hunt.

The Coyote and His Prey

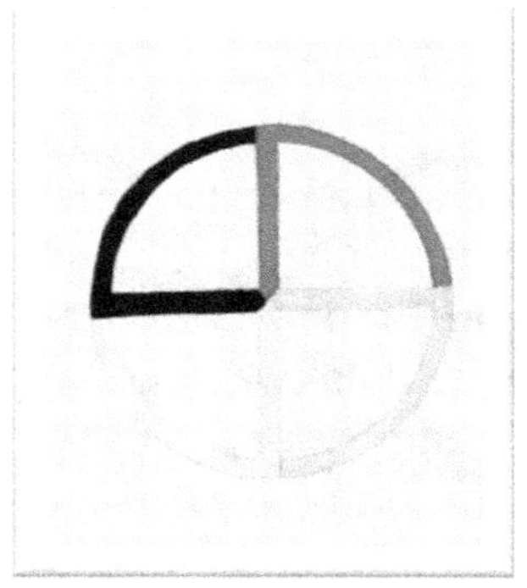

Aliksai! At Hohoyapi the people were living. The Coyote had children somewhere. So, he was hunting some food for them and had killed a rabbit and he did not want to eat it alone, so he mounted a bluff and called it out in the way Coyotes bark.

So, from the north came a yellow Coyote, from the west a blue one, from the south a red one, from the east a white, from the north east a black, and from the south east a gray one. "This here I killed," he said to, them, "and because I do not want to eat it alone, I have called you. We shall eat it together." So, they tore it to pieces and devoured it there very quickly, and that is the reason why a coyote never eats any prey that he has found alone, but always calls out when he has found something.

How The Circle (PÓNGO) Katcina and His Wife Became Stars

(Hopi)
The Traditions of the Hopi H. R. Voth [1905]

Halíksai! In Oraíbi the people were living. In the north-western part of the village was at that time a kiva called Hâmís-kiva. Somewhat south of this kiva close to the present site of the, Hanó-kiva lived a maiden. She persistently refused to marry any young man in the village. At Red Sand (Palánvisa), a place north-east of the village, some maidens were playing the game "jumping over the trays." The maiden mentioned above never played with the other maidens, but one time she went out intending to play with the maidens. When she came to the edge of the mesa she sat down and watched the other maidens play. A young man dressed in a blue Hopi blanket came by and asked her why she did not play with the other maidens. "Yes," she said, "I never play with them." Hereupon he sat down beside her and they talked together a little while, then the maiden returned to her home.

In the evening she was grinding corn. While she was grinding a Katcina came to the village, danced first near the Coyote (Ish) kiva, then at the Singer (Táo) kiva, then at the public plaza (Kíconvee), then at the Wrinkle (Wíkolapi) kiva, and finally at the Hâmís-kiva. Hereupon he left the village. The next morning the mána again proceeded to the place at the edge of the mesa where she had been sitting the previous day, and again the youth joined her. This time he asked her if she would marry him if her father and mother were willing. She consented. He told her that if they were willing, he would come and get her the next day. He then told her that he was the Katcina who was dancing in the village, saying that he would again dance at the same places as usual, and then after he would be through, she should come and meet him at "The Place-Where-Scalps-are-Dressed" (Yóvutzrhrokwanpi). Hereupon they parted.

In the evening she was again grinding corn and the Katcina again went through the village dancing at the places mentioned, and singing the following song while he was dancing, singing the same song at each place:

Achípolaina, achipolaina,
Koohochunisha, kowishkúnishaa,
Palainaiya ---------------- --aya.
Waa-i-aha-ihihi.

The mána had in the meanwhile obtained the permission of her parents to marry the youth. The mother filled a tray with meal for her, with which the mana proceeded to the place named by the Katcina. Here she was met by the Katcina after he had made his round through the village. From here they proceeded to the place called Kocántûika, a bluff named after a certain plant, kocána.

When they arrived here, they saw a kiva and a light in it. A voice called out from the kiva inviting them to come in. They entered and found here a great many different Katcinas. The youth was the Circle (Póngo) Katcina. Hereupon the youth handed the mána some píki made of fresh roasting ears, and also some watermelon slices, which she ate. They then remained in this kiva, the mána preparing the food for the Katcinas, and the latter preparing the bridal costume for the mána. Every night the Póngo Katcina would go to the village and dance, as already explained. When the bridal costume was finished the mána went home in the same manner in which brides go home to-day. Her husband followed her, so they lived in the house of her parents after that. Her parents now found out that the husband of their daughter was a Katcina.

By and by she bore two children, which were also Circle Katcinas. One time the young mother was drying corn-meal, stirring it in a pot over the fire. When she was done with this, she left her house and went to the edge of the mesa outside of the village. Her husband had gone to visit the Katcinas at the Katcina kiva mentioned before. While the woman was outside of the village some one approached her. It was the Hotóto Katcina. He told her that she should go with him, to which she consented. They descended the mesa south of the village and went southward to Shongópavi. When the Circle Katcina returned to the house he found his wife gone. Following her tracks, he found that she had gone away with some one, and soon heard who it was that had taken her away. He returned to the house, took his two children and went with them to the Katcina house already mentioned. Here they remained. The two little Katcinas learned the Katcina songs and dances.

After a while the father and his two children concluded to try to find the mother of the two youths. So, the people cooked some roasting ears and other food for them, whereupon they proceeded to the village, taking the food with them. Here they danced at Pisávi, a place a short distance east of the Pongóvi kiva. While they danced, they sang the following song:

Ahahahahai ahahaai
Ahahahaha ihihihihihi
Umungu uyungnaya
Umungu uchioli
Ahahahahai ihihihihi-hi-hi-hi.

When they were through singing, the father asked the women among the spectators whether some one would not nurse the children for these roasting ears that they had brought with them, but no one was willing. They went to the plaza, repeated their dancing and singing, whereupon the father again asked the women that some one nurse his children for the roasting ears, but no one was willing. They then proceeded to the Coyote kiva, where the same thing was repeated. No one being willing to nurse the two children, they left the village and when they came to the last row of houses, where the Katcinas often rest when they have dances now, a woman approached them declaring that she was willing to nurse the children. After she had nursed them and they had given her the roasting ears, they left the village along the trail leading south-eastward. Here they traced the mother to Sik'ákvu, a bluff on top of the mesa about three miles southeast of Oraíbi.

Here they found a kiva where they heard some one singing the following song:

Tciihiihihio tcihihiokaaha,
Tcihihiokaaha someone,
Ha, ha, ha!

It was the Haháii Wuhti, who was opening comíviki as she was singing. When they heard the song, they looked into the kiva and were noticed by the Haháii Wuhti. "Oh!" she said, "here I am meeting you with this song. Recently somebody was fetching your mother by here." The three went into the kiva and were invited to remain overnight. They were fed by the Haháii Wuhti the comíviki. When they had eaten, they danced, singing the following song:

Ahahahaihahaiiya toywihihiovohokahai,
Ahahaahaaiahaiya toywihihiovohokahai,
Ocarasotikiiihi, polaihainahai,
Kahaahaowkuruhukahai, koaowaikurukahaihai.

In the morning they proceeded eastward. In the evening of the next day, they arrived at a place called Owl Spring (Móngkba). Here they found another Haháii Wuhti in a kiva, who was also engaged in opening comíviki. She was singing the same song that the other Haháii Wuhti had been singing. When the three arrived, they looked into the kiva. When the woman noticed them, she said, "Utí! here you some one is going about and I am meeting you with this song. Recently some one fetched your mother by here." They went in and were fed by the Haháii Wuhti, whereupon they again danced and sang the same song which they sang at the place of the other Haháii Wuhti. They stayed overnight at this kiva., and during the night the Haháii Wuhti went to Kí'shiwuu, where many different kinds of Katcinas had a dance. When one party had danced and gone away, another party would come and perform their dance and leave. Then another party, and so on. When all had danced, Haháii Wuhti returned to her home and told the three Circle Katcinas about the dance. She told them about it; then they also went and performed a dance at Kí'shiwuu, which, it seems, was not far away. When they were through, they again returned to Móngkba. Here they remained until it became morning.

In the morning Haháii Wuhti again went to Kí'shiwuu to be present at another dance, the three Circle Katcinas remaining behind. When they had all danced Haháii Wuhti again Invited the three Katcinas. The people who had seen them in the last dance during the night and had not observed them during the day were waiting for them, thinking that they probably would come. They went over and also performed their dance. Before they went over Haháii Wuhti told them that their mother was at Kí'shiwuu and that she would see them dance and she would certainly be anxious to return with them. They performed their dance on the public plaza, singing the same song that they had sung at the places of the two Haháii Wuhtis, when they were through, they again returned and soon met their mother, who had recognized them and had gone before them. So, they took their mother back with them.

Before they reached Móngkba night befell them, so they stopped. The father said to the two children they should go ahead to their grandmother, the Haháii Wuhti, which they did. He then took a pointed stick and killed his wife with it by thrusting it into her throat. Leaving the body at the place, he followed his two sons, but before he reached the place where they were the skeleton of his wife followed him. The two boys had safely gotten into the house of their grandmother, but their father ran away, being followed by the skeleton. He finally arrived at the First Mesa, rushed into the village of Háno and there into a kiva where a number of women were making jugs. He begged them to hide him as something was pursuing him. Hereupon one of the women hid him under a pile of clay which they were using for making their pottery. The skeleton then arrived, saving, "Havá! Did my husband not come here?" she asked. "No," they replied. "Yes," the skeleton said, "because his tracks end here," and hereupon she entered the kiva. She threw aside all the piles of clay and material that was lying there, and finally came to the pile under which the man was hidden.

When he noticed that she was close by he jumped up, ran up the ladder and westward towards Wálpi, being pursued by the skeleton of his wife. In Wálpi he again entered a kiva. Here they were practicing a war dance. "Hide me quickly," he said, "some one is following me." "Come here," they said, and handed him a drum. So, he beat the drum. The skeleton soon arrived and entered the kiva after having spoken the same words as in Háno. She shoved the dancers aside, but when she came to the one who was beating the drum, he threw aside the drum and rushed out, running to Mishóngnovi. Here he again rushed into a kiva where they were assembled for the Lagón ceremony. The women were making trays. He again asked to be hidden as he was being pursued by some one. One of the women told him to be seated in her lap, which he did. She covered him with a tray that she was working on and continued her work. Soon the skeleton arrived, asked the same questions, and was again answered in the negative. She came in, looked around, driving the women from one place of the kiva into another, until she arrived at the one who had her husband. When he saw that he could not remain hidden he rushed out and ran towards Shongópavi. Here they also were assembled for the Lagón ceremony and the same thing was repeated that took place in Mishóngnovi.

From here he ran towards Matö'vi (about fifteen miles south of Shongópavi). At this place the Flute society had a ceremony. They were assembled at the spring when he arrived, He again repeated the same request to be hidden, as he was being pursued. They told him to go into the spring to a certain sunflower stalk that was growing in the spring. This he should mount and hide in its top. He did so. When the skeleton arrived and asked whether her husband was not there the Flute priest told her, "Yes, he has entered the spring." So, she went to the edge of that spring and entered it. Looking into the water she saw the sunflower stalk reflected in the water and on top of it her husband. Thinking that he was in the water she dived in and disappeared.

The pursued man came down and joined the Flute players. On the fourth day they heard somebody pound yucca roots in the water. When the sun rose, the woman came out of the water, dressed in a bridal costume, and carrying in her arms a reed receptacle which contained another bridal robe and the white belt. She appeared in exactly the same manner as the newly married bride appears on the morning when she returns from the home of her husband to that of her own mother. When she came out the two priests called the two together, placed them back-to-back, made a road with sacred meal for each one; the one road southward, and the other northward. The priests told them to proceed four steps, each one in the direction they were facing. Then they should turn and meet again. But the man returned when he had taken three steps instead of four. The Flute priests were very angry and called at the woman to run. She started, and her husband started after her. "You shall always follow each other this way," the Flute priests said. They both ran westward, and are still running in that way. The two stars, Nangö'sohu pursue each other because one constantly follows the other, sometimes overtaking it and then again remaining behind, are these two personages.

When the Coyote Married the Maiden

(Navaho)
The Dîné: Origin Myths
of the Navaho Indians
Aileen O'Bryan

After the first loom was made the people lived peacefully for about half a century. Then these strange creatures that were born began to eat the people. There is a little hill called tqnts'i'se ko just across the Mancos Canyon, which used to be a house. It was the home of 12 brothers. (On the top of this hill you can see a ruin.) The brothers were great hunters and hunted all over the mesas. They had one sister. The girl grew to be a beautiful maiden, and the holy men came from far and wide to ask her to marry them.

The maiden's name was Ataed'diy ini. When her brothers were away hunting, she stayed at home alone. Now the Coyote came to the brothers and called out: "Brothers-in-law." He wanted this maiden to become his wife. Ataed'diy ini told him "No," for only the one who killed the giant would become her husband. The Coyote sat there with his head down for a moment, then he said: "Very well." He left her and went to the home of the giant.

When he saw the giant, he said: "Brother, why do people outrun you? Now if you want me to, I can make you run as fast as I can. I have no trouble getting meat. I know of herbs that will clean your system; and I will show you the medicine which I use on my legs to make me run fast."

Now this giant was very clumsy; he just walked along slowly and when people saw him, they became so frightened that they were unable to run away. Because of this he could pick them up and put them in his big basket. The giant was, however, interested in the Coyote's plan.

The Coyote told the giant to build a sweat house; and while the giant was doing this the Coyote gathered the herbs. He also got a fresh leg of deer. When the sweat house was built and the hot stones placed inside, they both entered it. Each took a good drink of the herb infusion the Coyote prepared. Now the drink made them nauseated and they vomited into the bowls each had taken into the sweat house. In the Coyote's bowl were found grasshoppers and lizards; the giant had vomited fat meat; but the Coyote hastily changed the bowls, and pulling aside the door covering and letting in the light, he showed them to the giant and said: "Look what you vomited. These things keep you from running swiftly". The giant said: "I see." They left the sweat house to get cool.

"Now," said the Coyote, "I will give you the medicine for your legs so that you will run swiftly." It was well with the giant. They returned to the sweat house; and the Coyote secretly took the deer's leg with him. The Coyote said: "Now comes the last step. This is very powerful medicine that I use." In the darkness he laid the deer's leg over his own leg and cut it in two. He put the giant's hand over the severed leg and showed him that it was indeed in two pieces. The giant said: "I see." The Coyote then quickly put the pieces of the deer's leg back of himself. He commenced spitting on his own leg and said: "Now get well, get well." After this he made the giant feel his perfect leg. The Coyote told the giant that now all the bad food was out of his stomach, and all the bad blood was out of his leg, and that he could outrun anything he saw. The giant said again, "I see."

After this the Coyote got out his knife and said that he would do the same thing for the giant's leg. He out off one of them, and the giant groaned with great pain. The giant began to spit on the two parts. He tried to make them grow together. But the Coyote grabbed the giant's severed leg and ran away with it, saying: "I never heard of a bone growing together in a day."

The Coyote took the giant's leg to the maiden and told her that he had killed the giant. But the maiden said that before she would marry him, she would have to kill him; and if he could return to life, then he could be her husband. The Coyote hung his head and covered his eyes with his hand for a moment. "Very well," he said, and he went away.

He went a short distance to the east side of the dwelling, and there he formed a little black mountain. He put a tunnel through the mountain, and he traveled still farther to the east. He then took out his lungs and heart and wrapped them in the Black Wind. He returned through the tunnel to the maiden's home. He said: "Now you can do as you wish with me." She got a club and killed him and threw his body on the ash dump. She went into her house, but he followed her. "Are you my wife now?" he asked her. But she said: "I have to kill you twice." So, he left her and traveled to the south, and there be built a blue mountain, and he carved a tunnel through it. To the south be took out his heart and his lungs and he wrapped them in the Blue Wind. Only his body returned to the maiden's dwelling. He said: "Now do whatever you wish with me." So, she killed him and cut him into pieces and threw them. on the ash heap. But he followed her into her house and asked: "Are you my wife now?" But she said: "No, I must kill you three times." He left her and went out to the west, and there be built a yellow mountain; and he cut a tunnel through it; and in the west he left his heart and lungs wrapped in the Yellow Wind. He returned to the maiden and spoke to her as before. But again, she killed him and ground the carcass with earth and threw it out. She returned to the house but he followed her. He said: "Are you my wife now?" But she answered: "No, four times I must kill you." This time the Coyote went to the north and built a white mountain. He cut a tunnel, as before. At its end he left his heart and lungs wrapped in the White Wind. His body returned to the maiden. "Now do with me whatever you wish," he said. This time, after she killed him, she cut him into pieces, ground the pieces with earth and threw it in all directions. Satisfied, she returned to her home; but after a little while the Coyote came in and said: "Now are you my wife?" The maiden asked him how he could do these things. He told her that after she became his wife, he would show her his magic. She let the Coyote come. He became her husband and she became his wife. Then he took her to the east and showed her the mountain and the tunnel that he had made. And he took her to the south, and west, and north. She learned to do what the Coyote had done. He taught her his ways.

And now she was called Jikai'naazi'li, Tingling Maiden.

After a time, they saw the brothers returning. The two were frightened and did not know what to do. The Coyote jumped over a pile of goods (blankets) and his wife covered him. When the brothers entered the house, the fire was out, and the girl sat there looking strangely. She was not the same. The eldest brother asked in surprise: "Why is the fire out? Why is there nothing cooking? Why is the home not in order?"

The eldest brother told the others to get wood. The brothers did this and built a fire of cedar wood. When the fire was burning the odor of coyote was strong inside the house. The eldest brother told the others to throw out the wood and to bring fresh wood. A second fire was built of fresh wood, but still they smelled coyote. They threw the firewood out again and they gathered the branches of trees, but it did no good; they gathered the topmost branches, but still the odor of coyote was strong in the dwelling. The eldest brother then cursed the coyote. "The Coyote with his ugly odor is everywhere," he said. Just then the Coyote threw the cover off and came out, saying: "What is the trouble, my brothers-in-law?"

Now the brothers did not know what to say. They sat around the fire with their heads down. In a short time, they went out and built themselves a little shelter, and they camped there that night. The house they left for the Coyote and his wife.

The following morning when the brothers went out to hunt, the Coyote said that he would go with them. The eldest brother told the others that from then on, they could only expect trouble. "But it is our duty to hunt," he said, "and we must go and hunt today."

Now in those days all was sacred and holy. There was a rainbow, formed like a young man, lying by the canyon's edge. They threw him over the canyon and crossed on him. After the brothers had crossed the canyon, they heard the Coyote calling far behind them. The eldest brother said: "I guess that we had better bring him across before he does something worse than howling." So, they went back and brought him over the rainbow.

They were on a mesa north of the Mancos Canyon when the Coyote came chasing a big ram. (There were many mountain sheep there at that time.) One of the brothers pulled his bow and aimed his arrow at the ram. He shot the arrow and killed the ram. Now in those days the horn of the mountain sheep was filled with fat, delicious marrow; and all the hunters prized it as their favorite fat. Whoever killed a sheep, to him went the horns. When the Coyote saw that the ram, he had been chasing had been killed by one of the brothers he claimed the horns. The brother spoke to the Coyote and told him to behave like a man once in a while. "There was a rule that whoever kills a sheep gets the horns." With this the brother began to cut the pair of horns. The Coyote stood to one side and whispered: "Turn to bone. Turn to bone." The brother cut and cut, but the horn had turned to solid bone. And where he had tried to cut it ridges formed. That is why there, are rings on mountain sheep horns today.'

The brothers dressed the sheep and rolled the meat into a little ball. They told the Coyote to take the meat to his wife and to tell her to have it ready for them when they returned. One of the brothers took the Coyote across the canyon. He warned him by no means to put the meat ball down on the way. But no sooner had the brother departed than he put down the meat ball. Immediately it turned into the big pile of meat. The Coyote thought that he could do what the brothers had done. He tried to roll it into a little ball again; but he could not do it. He walked over to the canyon's edge and he saw that way down in the bottom of the canyon a big game was going on. There were people in the canyon playing this game. They were the Swallow People or cliff dwellers. The Coyote called down to them; he said that they were certainly an ugly people--the man and their wives alike. He said that his wife was beautiful and light of skin.

All this made the cliff people very angry, and they decided to get rid of him, to kill him. While the Coyote sat up there calling out insults, two young spider men climbed up the wall of the canyon; and from the cliff's edge they spun a long, high fence strong as woven mats. It was very high and very strong, and it extended for a long way back of the Coyote. After the two young men had finished, they returned to the bottom of the canyon. Then all the cliff people went after the Coyote who was still sitting there on the rim mocking them. He insulted them and he kicked at them and he said that not one in all that crowd could catch him. Just as they reached the rim of the canyon, away he went as fast as he could run. But he came up against the spider men's fence and it threw him back, He tried to jump over it but failed. Now, the cliff people were very near. He tried and tried to jump over the fence, and the fourth time he fell back among the cliff people. They caught him and killed him. They cut his hide into strips and made headbands of the fur. That is why swallows have a little ring around their heads. They have worn these little light bands ever since they made them out of the Coyote's hide.

The Maiden and the Coyote

(Oraibi)
Told by Qoyawaima

A long time ago a beautiful maiden lived in the northern part of the village of Oraibi. The young men of the village vied with one another to gain her favor, but she treated with contempt all attempts in that direction. The young men would gather flowers, some of them even going long distances to find rare flowers, and offer them to her, but she would persistently refuse to accept any of them. So, they finally gave up the attempts in disgust.

The Yellow Cloud chief of the north heard about it and also decided to try to win her. He prepared a beautiful bridal outfit, consisting of two robes, a pair of moccasins, a knotted belt, and a reed mat, the latter to be used as a receptacle for a part of the outfit. In fact, it was the same outfit that is made for brides at the present time, but yellow being the color of the north with the Hopi, this whole outfit was of that color. The chief brought it to the village and presented it to the maiden, but she refused to accept it, so he, too, returned to his home in disgust. The Blue Cloud chief of the west hearing about this, made up his mind that he would try to win the favor of that maiden, so he prepared a blue bridal outfit and offered it to the maiden, but it was promptly refused. Hereupon the Red Cloud chief of the south prepared the same outfit in red color, but also without success. The White Cloud chief of the east tried his luck with a white bridal costume, but with no better results. The Black Cloud chief from above failed in the same manner, and finally the Gray Cloud chief from below tried his luck, only to meet with complete failure, as his five companions had.

After all these attempts and failures, Pavayoyk'ashi, a rain deity in the far south, heard about this story. He painted and dressed up beautifully like the Flute players, Powamuy dancers, and certain Katcinas at the present day, painted a black line over his cheeks and nose, took a bow and arrows, placed the latter in a panther skin quiver and proceeded to Oraibi. He found the maiden already mentioned, in the valley south of Oraibi watching her father's field, He addressed her, saving, that she should speak to her parents and ask them whether they would give her to him and, in case they should give their consent, he would come and get her in four days. She was favorably impressed with him and promised to do so. In the evening, when she arrived in her home, she told her parents about it, saying that somebody had come there, had asked her in marriage provided they, the parents, would give their consent. The parents offered no objections.

The Coyote Old Man at that time lived west of the village at a place called Coyote Gap. He had been thinking of that maiden, but knowing that she had refused all offers, had never had the courage to ask for her. Hearing now that she had accepted Pavayoyk'ashi, he at once determined to win her. So, he traveled south to a country where it is warm and where there are parrots and macaws. He captured one of the macaws, returned, and at once proceeded to the house of the maiden, saving: "I have brought something pretty for you." She asked, "What is it?" He produced the parrot and asked her whether she wanted it. She was at once struck with the beauty of the bird, and, not thinking of any evil intentions that the Coyote might have, accepted the present. The parrot was alive. The Coyote, well pleased with his success, returned to his house. During the night he proceeded to the house of Pavayoyk'ashi, stole his costume and ornaments and all that he usually took with him, and returned.

The next morning, he dressed and painted up just like Pavayoyk'ashi and proceeded to the house of the maiden, this being the day on which Pavayoyk'ashi had said that he would come for her, she mistook Coyote Old Man for her lover and went with him. They proceeded to the house of the Coyote Old Man where she remained. She soon discovered her mistake and was very unhappy over it.

When Pavayoyk'ashi awoke in the morning, he missed his costume. After hunting for it and being unable to find anything, he discovered tracks leading to and from his house. He followed these and tracked them to the house of the maiden, from there back to the house of the Coyote, where to his great sorrow he found her. He did not say anything, however, but returned to his home, being, of course, very angry.

In the meanwhile, the young men of the village heard that the beautiful maiden, whom to win they had made so many unsuccessful attempts, had been ensnared by the Coyote Old Man. They were very much exasperated over it, went down the mesa, surrounded the Coyote's house and determined to kill the Coyote. When they arrived there, he was still sleeping. The maiden, sitting by his side, was very much dejected. When the Coyote heard the noise he awoke, jumped up, ran up the ladder and succeeded in escaping between and through the pursuers without being hurt by the sticks that were hurled at him. Ascending a ridge or mesa some distance west of the village, he turned around and in a defiant way expressed his satisfaction at the victory he had gained over them, by successfully getting their most beautiful maiden away from them, and the village. Then descended the mesa upon the other side and disappeared.

Pavayoyk'ashi bided his time and one time brought a strong wind, some very heavy rain and thunder clouds, in which he was hidden, to the village. He took revenge on his enemy, the Coyote, by striking him dead with a ray of lightning. The maiden returned to her home, but realizing that she had cast herself away, she continued to lead a life of lewdness.

Story of the Lost Wife

(Sioux)
Myths and Legends of the Sioux McLaughlin, Marie L. (1916)

A Dakota girl married a man who promised to treat her kindly, but he did not keep his word. He was unreasonable, fault-finding, and often beat her. Frantic with his cruelty, she ran away. The whole village turned out to search for her, but no trace of the missing wife was to be found.

Meanwhile, the fleeing woman had wandered about all that day and the next night. The next day she met a man, who asked her who she was. She did not know it, but he was not really a man, but the chief of the wolves.

"Come with me," he said, and he led her to a large village. She was amazed to see here many wolves -- gray and black, timber wolves and coyotes. It seemed as if all the wolves in the world were there.

The wolf chief led the young woman to a great tepee and invited her in. He asked her what she ate for food.

"Buffalo meat," she answered.

He called two coyotes and bade them bring what the young woman wanted. They bounded away and soon returned with the shoulder of a fresh-killed buffalo calf.

"How do you prepare it for eating?" asked the wolf chief.

"By boiling," answered the young woman.

Again, he called the two coyotes. Away they bounded and soon brought into the tent a small bundle.

In it were punk, flint and steel -- stolen, it may be, from some camp of men.

"How do you make the meat ready?" asked the wolf chief.

"I cut it into slices," answered the young woman.

The coyotes were called and in a short time fetched in a knife in its sheath. The young woman cut up the calf's shoulder into slices and ate it.

Thus, she lived for a year, all the wolves being very kind to her. At the end of that time the wolf chief said to her:

"Your people are going off on a buffalo hunt. Tomorrow at noon they will be here. You must then go out and meet them or they will fall on us and kill us."

The next day at about noon the young woman went to the top of a neighboring knoll. Coming toward her were some young men riding on their ponies. She stood up and held her hands so that they could see her. They wondered who she was, and when they were close by gazed at her closely.

"A year ago, we lost a young woman; if you are she, where have you been," they asked.

"I have been in the wolves' village. Do not harm them," she answered.

"We will ride back and tell the people," They said. "Tomorrow again at noon, we shall meet you."

The young woman went back to the wolf village, and the next day went again to a neighboring knoll, though to a different one. Soon she saw the camp coming in a long line over the prairie. First were the warriors, then the women and tents.

The young woman's father and mother were overjoyed to see her. But when they came near her the young woman fainted, for she could not now bear the smell of human kind. When she came to herself, she said:

"You must go on a buffalo hunt, my father and all the hunters. Tomorrow you must come again, bringing with you the tongues and choice pieces of the kill."

This he promised to do; and all the men of the camp mounted their ponies and they had a great hunt. The next day they returned with their ponies laden with the buffalo meat. The young woman bade them pile the meat in a great heap between two hills which she pointed out to them. There was so much meat that the tops of the two hills were bridged level between by the meat pile. In the center of the pile the young woman planted a pole with a red flag. She then began to howl like a wolf, loudly.

In a moment the earth seemed covered with wolves. They fell greedily on the meat pile and in a short time had eaten the last scrap.

The young woman then joined her own people.

Her husband wanted her to come and live with him again. For a long time, she refused. However, at last they became reconciled.

The Coyote and the Turtles

(Oraibi)
Told by Qoyawaima

A long time ago the Turtles lived in a river called Blue River (Sakwabayu), somewhere south-east of Winslow (Homolovi). The Coyote was always hunting for something to eat. One time he was also hunting for food near the place where the Turtles lived. The latter would sometimes come out of the water and hunt cactus (yo'ngo) which they relished very much, and from which they have their name, Yongo'sona (pl. Yoyo'ngosontu).

One of the Turtles had a little baby Turtle. One time when they were all going to hunt food again, the Turtle said: "I am not going to take my child with me, because it is sleeping so nicely. I am going to bring a cactus back with me and give it to my child." After they had left, the little Turtle awoke, and when it found nobody there it asked, "Where is my mother?" and began to cry, and at once came out of the water. Looking for the tracks, it found that they led to the bank and then way off somewhere. It followed the tracks for some distance, but could not find any one, and so cried very bitterly. The Coyote, hearing the cries of the little Turtle, at once hunted it up and when he found it, he said: "What are you singing? You are singing something very nice. Sing again." "I am not singing," the little Turtle said, "but I am crying." "What are you crying for?" the Coyote asked. "My mother has gone away and did not take me along," the Turtle replied, and continued to as follows:

Tingaoco, tingaoco, Waoo, waoo, h-h-h-h (these h's spoken in quick succession while inhaling, to imitate the sobbing of a child that is sometimes heard in connection with or rather after a cry).

The Coyote again urged the Turtle to sing, as he called the crying, saying: "If you do not sing, I am going to devour you." The little Turtle was very much afraid, but refused to comply with the request of the Coyote. The Coyote repeated his threat, saving, "I shall certainly devour you if you do not sing." The little Turtle, thinking of the subterfuge said: "All right, it will not hurt me; I will then simply live in your body," The Coyote said to himself, "Maybe the Turtle will continue to live in my body and move about there." And so, he repeated his request, but this time changing his threat. "If you do not sing," he said, "I am going to throw you in that water there." "Don't do that, because if you do, I shall drown," The Coyote did not know that the little Turtle lived in the water, and that he was being imposed upon. "All right," he said, "I shall not throw you in the water, but I shall devour you," and thereupon he took hold of the Turtle and ran towards the water. Arriving at the bank he slung the little Turtle away into the midst of the water.

"Aha! My house (Ali, Ikiningwu)," said the Turtle, and then dived into the water, but immediately came out again, saving, "Aha! My house. Thanks that you have brought me here (Ali, Ikiningwu! kwakwa, um nui pak wiki)," and, swimming around on the water, laughed at the Coyote.

The Coyote was very angry and said: "Oh! That, I did not devour you; but I am going to hunt your mother now, and if I find her somewhere, I shall certainly devour her," and thereupon ran away.

Following the tracks of the Turtles, he met them on their way back to the water. They had been away quite a distance, had eaten there to their hearts' content, and were now returning. When the Coyote met them, he said to the first one, "I am going to devour you," and tried to seize it.

The Turtle immediately drew its head, feet and tail into the shell, and thus the Coyote, although he was working around it, throwing it over, pushing it backward and forward a long time, could not hurt it. He got very angry and jumped towards another one with the same result; so, he tried others, but when he found that he could not hurt them, nor break their shell, he left them in disgust.

When the Turtles arrived home, the Turtle mother gave a cactus to her child, saying: "This I brought for you," and the child ate it in great delight. "When did you awake?" the mother asked. "About half-way noon I woke up, and when I found that you were all gone, I cried." "Yes," the mother said, "you were sleeping so nicely, and so I did not take you along."

The little Turtle then related everything about the Coyote, saying that the latter had threatened to devour it, but when he had been told that he could just do so, and that the little Turtle would then live in his body, he desisted. The Turtle mother laughed at it. The child then continued to relate how the Coyote had asked it to sing, and when refused he threatened to throw it into the water, and that he had done so, although the child had said that it would certainly drown; and the child continued, "When he threw me into the water, I laughed at him and told him, 'Here I am living'; and so, I got back without even getting tired."

The mother laughed at it and was very happy, saying: "Thanks that he brought you here, and that you got home even without becoming tired." And the Turtles are living there in that water still.

The Water Serpent and the Coyote

(Oraibi)
Told by Qoyawaima

Listen! The people were here living (Aliksai! Yao yep yeshiwa). The Water Serpent (Balolookong) was living in Lanva, the Flute Spring, and a short distance towards the south at Ishmovala the Coyote was living. They were strong friends and often visited each other. They were still young, but the Water Serpent was already very long so that when he visited the Coyote and coiled up in his kiva he filled the entire kiva, leaving only a very small place for the Coyote, near the fireplace, where he had to sit in a crouched position. "I am going to be still larger," the Water Serpent said to him one time, "so you must enlarge your kiva." He then invited the Coyote to visit him once too, which the Coyote promised to do.

He meditated how he, too, could fill the kiva of the Water Serpent and said to the Snake: "I am going to become large and my tail will become long some day, too." While he said this the Snake was already slowly leaving the kiva, but he was so long that when the head was out already, a large part of the body was still in the kiva. After he had left, the Coyote said to himself: "Now, let me go and hunt something, too." In the evening he left the kiva and went to a place where a great deal of cedar grew. Here he pulled off a large bundle of cedar bark and carried it home. "How shall I make a tail now?" he said to himself. Soon he began to rub the cedar bark so as to make it pliable, and laying it out on the floor in a long line, wrapped it up with yucca leaves, which he had also brought with him. "But how shall I make this tail so that the Snake will not know, it?" he again asked himself, but soon formed a plan. He pulled out a lot of his hair and pasted it to the cedar bark so that it looked like a tail. This false tail he then fastened to his own tail.

In the morning when he had had his breakfast he went over to his friend, the Water Serpent. The latter had a larger kiva, so that there was sonic vacant space in it. When the Coyote had entered, he kept going around the kiva dragging his long tail after him. Then he kept circling around until the kiva also was well filled, and he sat down by the head of the Water Serpent and they talked with one another. The Water Serpent smiled, thinking to himself: "Well, that tail did not used to be this way, how can that be?" After they had talked together nearly all forenoon, the Coyote said he was going home to eat his dinner, and, uncoiling his long tail, he went up the ladder, saying to the Snake: "Now, whenever you feel that way, come and visit me too again sometime," which the Snake promised to do. As the Coyote went over to his kiva dragging his long tail after him, he looked around and smilingly said to himself, "Aha, he did not find out, because he did not say anything about my tail," When he came into his kiva, he went around coiling up his tail, and then untied it from his natural tail.

By and by the Snake went over to visit his friend, the Coyote, again. The latter, who had been looking for this visit, had been very much concerned about it, fearing that his friend might all at once come when he had his tail detached from his natural tail, and so was always on the lookout. Hence, he saw his friend coming, and had time enough to put his tail in order again, and when the Snake arrived at the kiva he was sitting at the fireplace, ready to receive his friend. The latter began to enter, but as he had been growing considerably since his last visit, and a part of the kiva was filled with the Coyote's tail, he did not find room enough for his whole body.

"I have been growing since I have been here last, and cannot get into this kiva now." "All right, let me go out," the Coyote said, "and I can talk to you from the outside while you are in the kiva. You might get cold out there."

So, the Coyote went out, circled around a number of times outside the kiva, coiling up his tail, and then took a seat near the kiva opening, conversing with his friend, the Water Serpent. By and by he got cold and began to wish that his friend would go home, but the latter remained.

The Coyote finally got very cold and began to be secretly angry at his friend because he tarried so long. At last, the latter said: "Now I must go home and eat my dinner." The Snake had not yet entirely left the kiva when the Coyote, who was very cold, rushed in and warmed himself. He was out of humor about the matter, and made up his mind to try to get even with his friend. "I am going to pay him back," he said to himself.

So, after he had eaten his dinner, he thought a great deal about the matter, and in the evening went to the timber again. He brought another armful of dry cedar bark and some yucca, and made another long addition to his tail in the same manner as before, only this time he made it considerably thicker. When it was done it filled his kiva entirely. He had so well covered it with hair and wool from his body that he thought nobody would know that it was not natural.

As the Snake had invited the Coyote at his last visit to visit him. Too, sometime again, the Coyote planned to go over to his friend, but thought he would wait until there was a cold day. As in about four days it became very cold, he concluded to pay his friend a visit.

Coming over to the kiva of the Snake, the two exchanged the usual greeting, the Coyote saying, "How! (is) the friend at home?" (How! kwatch katu?) "Yes, I (am) at home. Come in." (Owe! Pai nu katu. Paki!) Whereupon the Coyote entered the kiva, and kept circling around and around, filling the entire kiva with his tail. "Well!" the Snake said, "You are going to fill this whole kiva, so let me go outside and talk to you from there."

Leaving the kiva, the Water Serpent kept going around outside for some time, coiling up in such a manner that finally the head was close to the entrance so that he could talk with his friend. It was very cold and the Coyote smilingly thought to himself while he was feeling very comfortable in the warm kiva, "Now you can freeze out there, too." The Snake became very cold and wished that his friend might leave, but he tarried.

The Snake was shivering and became angry and wished very much that the Coyote might take his leave. Finally, the latter said that he must now go home and eat his dinner, and while the Coyote was going up the ladder dragging his tail after him, the Water Serpent went in. Arriving at the fireplace the latter said, "I am going to get even with you. I am going to pay you back;" and grabbing a stick at the fireplace, he shoved the part of the Coyote's tail that was still in the kiva on the fire, so that it caught fire, saying: "You get out of this; you (referring to the Coyote) are always taking other people's things and are always doing something bad; you had better get away from here."

The Coyote had by this time gotten away quite a distance, and, looking around, he admired his long tail. When he had nearly reached his kiva, he looked around again and then noticed some smoke and fire behind him, but as there was high grass around there at that time, he thought it was the grass burning. "Oh," he said, "the Hopi have set the grass on fire. They are after me and want to drive me away. Maybe they will kill me. I am not going to my house, but I am going to run away."

So, he began to run westward. Looking back, he again noticed the grass burning at various places and thought he was pursued. He finally reached the timber and when he saw that burning after a while, he concluded that he would run to Little Colorado River (Bayupa) and jump in there. Then he thought the people would not find him. He did not 'yet know at this time that his tail was burning. Arriving at the river, which was very high, he jumped in and tried to swim across, but before he got across, he became very tired. The river was drifting him along, and he finally sank down and drowned. The Balolookong now lived in peace at the spring forever afterwards.

The Coyote and the Hummingbird

(Oraibi)
Told by Kwayeshva

Ishyaoi! The Coyote was living at Ishmovala, west of Oraibi, and a Humming-bird was living at Tohchipchook'pu. They both had children and were good friends. One time the Coyote went to visit his friend, and as he also wanted to find some food for his children, he went north of the village to the place where the refuse of the village was thrown, and looked for some pieces of skin, old moccasins, remnants of hides, etc. The bird seeing it, went to a place close by and quickly buried itself so that the bill only was protruding.

When the Coyote came to the place where the bird had buried itself, he saw something protruding from the pile of debris and said: "Thanks, I have found a needle. I shall take that home to my mother and will sew a dress for herself." So, he took hold of the bill of the Humming-bird and began to pull at it. "Ishana!" the bird said, "that is my bill," and the Coyote saw that he had been fooled by his friend. The latter laughed at him.

They then went to the house of the bird, the latter entering the nest, which was built in the side of the bluff. As the Coyote could not get there, he sat on top of the bluff, and they conversed with each other. When it was nearly evening the Coyote said: "I must go home, it is evening. To-morrow you must visit me too." "All right," the Humming-bird said: "to-morrow I will come."

So, they slept that night, and in the morning, after they had eaten, the bird went over to the house of the Coyote; first, however, hunting some worms in fields near by. After having eaten a number of them it went over to the Coyote's house, and saw something protruding from the ground close to the house. "Thanks, I have found a gourd jug. I am going to take this home and when my mother pops corn she will put it in here and I will eat it out of this." Hereupon she commenced pulling at the supposed jug. "Ishana!" the Coyote said, "that is my snout." Hereupon they went to the Coyote's house. That having a large entrance, the bird, of course, could go in too. The Coyote fed his friend juniper berries (lapoci), the Coyote also eating some. After they had talked a while the Humming-bird returned to her home, and the two are probably still living there.

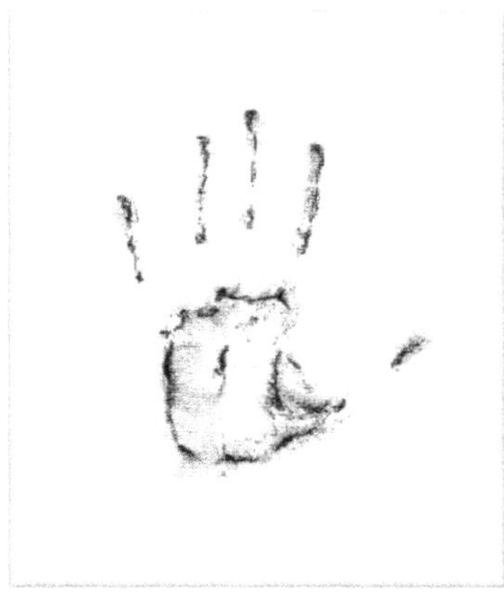

The Coyote and the Turtle-dove

(Shupaulavi)
Told by Lomavantiwa

Aliksai! The Shongopavi were living in their village, and South of the village there was a hill called Kwakchomo. There was a great deal of this grass called kwakwi there. A Turtle-dove one time was rubbing out the seed from the tassels of this grass, and while doing so cut her hand with the sharp edge of one of the blades of grass. It bled profusely, and the Turtle-dove was moaning as follows:

Hooho, hoo, hooho, hoo, hooho, hoo,
Ho-ho-ho-

While she was moaning a Coyote came along and heard somebody singing, as he believed. So, he approached the place. When he arrived at the place he saw the Turtle-dove sitting and leaning forward in deep distress. "Are you singing?" he asked the Dove. "Are you thus singing?" "No," she said, "I am not singing; I am crying. I have cut myself." "No, you are singing," the Coyote replied. "Now you sing to me." "No," the Dove insisted, "I was crying," thus refusing to confirm the Coyote's statements. "Now, if you are not willing to sing to me, I shall devour you," the Coyote said. The Dove then yielded and sang the above song again. The Coyote then imitating the song of the Dove, left her and ran away.

As he was running, he stumbled over a rock and fell down. As he fell, he lost the song, so that he was only able to say, "Ho-ho-ho." So, the Coyote made up his mind to go back again to the Turtle-dove, and, arriving at the place where she was sitting, he began to urge her to sing. "But I am not singing," She said, "I am crying." But he would not listen, so she again sang her song to him.

He again ran back, singing the Turtle-dove's song as he was running. Again, he stumbled over a rock and lost the song. He again tried to sing, but could only say, "Ho-ho-ho." So, he again returned to the place where the Turtle-dove had been, but the latter had gone immediately after the Coyote had left her, leaving at the place where she had been sitting a stone which very much resembled her form, and was also placed in about the position in which the Dove had been sitting.

"I have fallen down again and have forgotten my song, so I came back again," the Coyote said, but he received no reply. "If you do not sing, I am going to devour you," and again receiving no reply, he grabbed what he believed to be the Dove, but found that it was a stone.

He broke all his teeth, and much blood was streaming from his mouth. He at once ran back and taking his way towards Shupaulavi, came to the spring Toriva, which he approached in order to drink. As he put his mouth to the water, he saw a bloody face staring at him from the depth of the water.

Not knowing what it was, he did not dare to drink, and ran away. Making his way northward, he ran to another spring by the name of Nankava, which is situated north of Shupaulavi. Here he again saw his reflection in the water, and did not dare to drink. He then ran to a third spring by the name of Ishk'achokpu. Seeing the same reflection in the water again, he was angry and gnarled, or rather belched, at it, from which the spring has derived its name, the Coyote Belching Water.

He again was afraid to drink, but was very tired and thirsty by this time. "I am going to run to Oraibi," he said to himself; "there is a place where there is some water, and I believe there is nobody living in that place."

So, he ran to a place south-east of Oraibi, called Kuritvahchikpu. When he arrived at this place, he again put his snout to the water, and was just about to drink when he discovered a skeleton staring at him from the water. This time he was very angry and tore up the rocks around the spring, from which that place has derived its name. He by this time was so thirsty and exhausted that he fell down and died there.

The Coyote and the Blue Jays

(Oraibi)
Told by Wikvaya

Haliksai! A long time ago the people lived in Oraibi. West of the village, at Ishmovala, lived the Coyote and his wife. They had six children and the Coyote used to go and hunt rabbits for his children. One day he went hunting again and found a little cottontail rabbit, which he chased. The rabbit ran into the hole, which the Coyote could not enter. "How shall I get this rabbit out now?" he thought to himself; then somebody came along; it was the Badger. "You get this out for me here," the Coyote said, "I want this rabbit for my children to eat." So, the Coyote sat down and waited while the Badger scratched a hole until he reached the rabbit, whereupon he pulled the latter out. The Coyote was very happy. "Thus," he said, "on your account my children will have something to eat." Then the Coyote took the rabbit in his mouth and ran home with it, being very happy. When he arrived in his home the little Coyotes wrangled over the rabbit, tore it to pieces and devoured it, some of them getting something, others not, so they remained hungry.

The next morning both the Coyote and his wife went out in search of food again, the latter ascending up to the village, and ran past the village on the west side, then by the north side, turning northward over the mesas. Not finding anything, she finally entered the woods north of the village. All at once she heard something in the trees, and, looking up, she saw some Blue Jays in the tree. The Blue jays were dancing in the tree and she coveted them. They said to the Coyote: "We are having a dance here, you come and be with us and assist us." "I would like to," the Coyote said, "but how shall I get up there?" "Why, we shall lend you some of our wings, tails, and feathers," the Blue Jays said. "All right," she said. So, they took off some of their wings, tails, and feathers and put them on her legs. They then told her that she must dance and sing just the same as they did, and then they again began to sing.

The Coyote now having wings ascended and danced with them. When they had finished the song, they all flew away, the Coyote with them, and alighted on some other tree. This they repeated in all three times. They then flew up high into the air, the Coyote with them, and when they were very high up, they all surrounded the Coyote, each one saying: "This is my tail, this is my wing, these are my feathers," and then tore out all the feathers that they had loaned the Coyote. When they had torn out all the feathers the Coyote began to fall downward to the earth. When she reached it, she was dead.

Her children still had nothing to eat. When the Coyote father saw that his wife was not coming home, he concluded that he would go and hunt her. Following her tracks, he ascended to the village, passed the village on the west side, and when he reached the north side of the village the dogs of the village noticed him and pursued him. He at once left the footprints of his wife and ran back to his children. So, after that the little Coyotes had no mother. The Coyote then afterwards hunted food alone for his children, and that is the reason why so many Coyotes have to look out for their food alone.

The Coyote and the Eagle

Aliksai! North of Shupaulavi is the Katcina House (Katcinki). West of this is a bluff, and on top of this bluff used to live an Eagle. One time the Coyote came along. "What are you wandering around for?" the Eagle asked. "Yes," the Coyote said. The Eagle was standing on one foot, having the other foot hidden in his feathers. The Coyote was wondering, and asked: "Why are you standing on one foot?" "Yes," the Eagle said, "I cut one leg off, and so I am standing on one foot." "Is that so?" the Coyote said, and was thinking. "I am envious at you," he said to the Eagle; "I shall try to stand on one leg too; but how did you cut your leg off, bow is that done?" "Why," the Eagle replied, "you just lay your leg across a stone and strike on it with a sharp stone and then it will be cut off, it does not hurt, and you need not be afraid."

So, the Coyote hunted for a sharp stone and there was another sharp stone with a sharp edge. He laid his right hind leg across the latter, raised the small sharp stone and cut off his leg. Hereupon the Eagle lowered his second leg, stretched out his wings, and laughed at the Coyote and said: "I have two legs, see here." "Oh!" the Coyote said, "I, poor one, that I thoughtlessly cut off my leg." And while the Eagle flew away the Coyote was crying, and, limping away, probably perished somewhere.

The Coyote and the Turkeys

(Oraibi)
Told by Kwayeshva

Haliksai! At Ishmovala the Coyote was living, and at Nuvatuk'aovi, a short distance east of Ishmovala, the Turkey lived. They both had children and were great friends, and often visited each other. One time when the Coyote came to the house of the Turkeys they fed him pinon nuts, which he relished very much. The little Turkeys were very nicely figured, and the Coyote enjoyed looking at them. He envied them for their beautiful feathers and was wondering how they were figured so nicely. As he looked at them, he stroked their bodies with a forepaw. "Yes," the Turkey mother said, "I baked these, my children. I put them into an oven and baked them, then I ate their meat, but I did not break any bones, nor did I bite into any bones. Them I left entirely unhurt. Early in the morning I put them into a tray, waved them up and down, singing the following song over them:

Pipichacha, pipichacha (archaic).
Talahoya, huwamu, itimu!
Wake up, please, my children!

Then I threw all the bones outside and there my children got alive again, and since then they are so beautifully figured." She was, of course, deceiving him. "Oh!" the

Coyote said; "yes, these are very pretty, and I shall do the same."

In the evening he returned to his house and early the next morning he went after wood. Returning with the wood, he heated his oven. He made the oven very hot, then took one of his children and pitied it, but the little Turkeys had been so pretty and he had so envied them for their pretty figuring, that he threw the little Coyote into the oven. Hereupon another one, and another one, as he had a great many children. He threw them into the oven until the oven was full. He placed a stone over the opening and plastered up the oven. While they were being baked in the oven, he ground some corn to make some hurushiki. So, in the evening he took them out of the oven and found them thoroughly baked. He took out one after another and then commenced to eat. They tasted very fine. He ate all the meat, but the bones he did not hurt. He did not break any, nor did he crush any with his teeth. Gathering the bones into a basket he went to sleep.

During the night the Turkey mother said to her children: "We had better flee away from here on account of your uncle, the Coyote, because he will be very angry and will certainly come and devour us." Hereupon she sent her children away to the San Francisco Mountains (near Flagstaff). She took the pelts, blankets, etc., in which they had been sleeping, and rolling some of the smaller ones up, placed them on the floor and covered them up so as to make them appear as if they were still sleeping, under the covering. Hereupon she followed her children.

The Coyote in the meanwhile got up once and looked whether the sun was not yet rising, but it was still dark. After a while he looked again and then the sun came out. He at once took the tray (tuchaiya) containing the bones of his children, went out with it, waved it up and down the way the Turkey Woman had shown him, and sang the song which she had told him she had sung over the bones of her children. Hereupon he also threw the bones away. But alas! nothing became alive, and only the bones were lying there. When he saw what had happened, he cried bitterly and became very angry. "I shall go over to the house of the Turkey," he said, "and shall certainly devour the little Turkeys too." Hereupon he went over to his friend's house, running very fast. When he came to the house, he at once entered and thought they were all sleeping nicely. He jumped upon their beds and grabbed what he believed to be the young Turkeys, but found that nobody was there. They had deceived him. "Ah," he said, "they have run away, but I shall certainly overtake them."

So, he rushed out, hunted up the tracks of the Turkeys and followed them running very fast. While the Coyote was following their tracks, the Turkeys had arrived at the Little Colorado River, but when they had crossed it, the little Turkeys were very tired. "I shall leave you here," their mother said, "and run ahead of you." But one of the little ones was crying very bitterly. The Turkey mother ran ahead to the San Francisco Mountains and informed the Turkeys living there about what had happened. "You that are strong come quickly and help us; the Coyote is following us and he will kill my children. You go quickly and get them." So, two of the Turkey men that were very strong came out and ran towards the place where the Turkey mother had left her children. The latter, however, remained because she was very tired.

The Coyote in the meanwhile found the little Turkeys and chasing them, said: "Aha, I shall devour you" (Ali kurzh nu umui cowani). The little Turkeys were running around and crying very bitterly. just as the Coyote was about to take one of the little Turkeys the two Turkey men came upon him, grabbed the little ones, of which there were two, took them on their backs and ran away with them. "Why do you take them away?" the Coyote cried. "I am hungry and I want to eat them. That is the reason why I followed them." But they did not listen, and as they were strong and the Coyote was very tired, he had to return to his home hungry. But before he got home, he died.

The Chiro and the Coyote

(Oraibi)
Told by Qoyawaima

In Oraibi the people were living. At Ishmovala the Coyote lived. Away over there at K'ahk'angwovakaavi lived a great many Chiros, and they were always dancing there.

One time the Coyote was walking about east of their village. The Chiros saw him as they were dancing. They were singing as follows:

Ishawu, ishawu, hohoongyanikay colmoki
Coyote, Coyote, to dance is longing,
Ishawu, oomii hongina,
Coyote upward dances,
Aatk'amii hongina,
Downward dances,
Machiwa, machiwa, chirorororo.
Is called, is called chirorororo.

The Coyote was looking at them and wanted to dance along. "Very well," the Chiros said to him, whereupon each one of them gave him some feathers; one some wing feathers, another some tail feathers, and so on. They made for the Coyote wings and a tail, and put small feathers into his body, whereupon the Coyote was very happy.

"Thanks," he said, "that you have made wings for me. I am going to dance with you now." Hereupon they danced, again singing the same song. The Coyote danced with them. Now they were flying upward somewhere, and arrived somewhere away high up. Now they crowded around the Coyote and said: "Why, this is my wing; why, this is my tail; why, these are my feathers;" some of them had given him these things, and now they took everything away from him, and alas! he began to descend. He arrived at the earth and died. The Chiros laughed at him. "Thanks," they said, "that you have died, because you very often do commit depredations on some one's property. That is why you were going about again."

The Coyote and the Porcupine
(Shupaulavi)
Told by Sik'ahpik'i

At some distance southwest of Walpi is a place called
Water Killing Hill (Baqoychomo), where there are still
some old ruins. A short distance north of this place is a
place called Skeleton Hill (Maschomo). At these two places
the people from Oraibi, Walpi, and the other villages rested
with their captives after they had destroyed Aoatovi, taking
with them many men, women, and children. Here at these
places, it is said, they extorted from their captives the
secrets of their ceremonies and altars, and after they had
learned everything from them, they killed a good many of
them, probably torturing some of them. Tradition says that
in some cases they cut women's breasts off and left them to
perish. From this killing of those captives these two places
have derived their names.

At the first named place the Porcupine used to live, a long
time ago, while the Coyote was living at the last named

place. One time the Coyote went to visit his friend, the Porcupine. "Sit down," the latter said. "All right," the Coyote said, and so they talked together a long time. When it was noon, the Porcupine said: "We are going to eat something. You build a fire;" so the Coyote built a large fire. When the Coyote had built the fire, the Porcupine said: "Now we are going to have something to eat." So, he drew a small pointed stick from his hair on the top of his head and thrust it into his nose. After he had done this repeatedly, blood and fat dropped out of his nose on the fire, where it was roasted. This he handed to the Coyote to eat. So, they were eating. "Aha," the Porcupine said: "thus I am preparing food." "Yes," the Coyote said, "we are happy."

So, after they had eaten, they conversed until evening; then the Coyote said, "I must go home now." "Very well," the Porcupine replied, "it is evening now," "But you must visit me too, to-morrow," the Coyote said, and thereupon left, the Porcupine saying laughingly, "You will have something good too, since you have seen it here." So, the next morning the Porcupine went over to his friend and there sure enough found that the Coyote also had a pointed stick thrust into his hair. When it was noon again the Porcupine also built a fire at his friend's kiva. "We are going to eat something fine," the Coyote said. So, the Coyote pulled out his stick, drew close up to the fire, bent over it, and also began to poke his nose with the stick, whereupon also blood, mixed with fat or tallow, began to come out. It covered the fire, and finally began to flow away, and wouldn't stop. The Coyote's nose was bleeding and bleeding, and finally he became exhausted and fell down.

The Porcupine, thinking that his friend had died, laughed, and without having eaten anything, left the kiva and went home. He was angry at his friend because he wanted to imitate him, and now was not successful. By and by the Coyote revived. The blood had stopped flowing, forming large hard pieces of coagulated blood and grease in front of his nose. He was very angry. "That friend of mine," he said, "that friend is the cause that this happened to me; he wanted it this way. I am going to devour him." So, after he had become strong again the next morning, he went over to his friend to attack him. When he arrived there, he looked down, and his friend looking up noticed the blood on his nose. "Well now, have you not died? I thought you had died, and that is the reason why I went away." "Yes," the Coyote said very roughly, "you have bewitched me. On your account I almost died, and now I have come over here to devour you." "No, no," the Porcupine said, "you are not going to devour me. Why, you are my friend, and a friend will not eat up his friend. No, indeed." Then he began to talk kindly to his friend saying: "Well, since you have not died, we will live together again." The Coyote then also quieted down and they conversed together amicably. They then lived there again as friends, the Coyote thinking that he would have a chance sometime to take revenge on the Porcupine.

The Coyote and the Badger

(Oraibi)
Told by
Kiwanhongva

Haliksai! In the village they were living, and south of La'nangva at Coyote Gap (Ishmovala) the Coyote was living. At Badger Gulch (Honancika), about one-eighth of a mile south-east of Oraibi, lived the Badger. These two were great friends with each other, and often visited each other. One time the Oraibi were cleaning out the spring of La'nangva, in which the maidens of the village assisted. They had taken their food along, which they placed near a rock not far from the spring. Towards evening the chief said: "Now get your food and let us eat." So, they spread blankets on the ground and placed the food on it and ate. After they were through, they went to the village.

The Coyote was sitting a short distance away watching the people as they ate, and envied them. Early the next morning he heard the crier announce another spring cleaning. As soon as the Coyote heard this announcement he ran over to his friend, the Badger. Arriving at the latter's house, he asked: "Is my friend in?" "Yes," the latter replied, "come in!" "Very well," the Coyote said, "but I am in a hurry. These Oraibi are going to clean the spring again and they have something very fine to eat there. Let us go over and take part in the eating, but do not be slow. Follow me soon." "Very well," the Badger said. Hereupon the Coyote left, the Badger soon following him. They entered the Coyote's house, and from there the Badger commenced to dig a hole towards the place where the food was, and after he had gone a little way he turned around, which is the custom, of the badgers. The Coyote noticed it and said: "Oh! you are turning back again." "Yes," the Badger replied, "that is the way I dig. We must not be alone in this." "Yes," the Coyote said, here is some one else close by. He digs straight ahead."

Hereupon the Coyote left his house and ran over to a place a short distance east of his house where the Mole (Mu'yi) lived. He entered the latter's house and said: "The people are cleaning the spring there and they have a great deal of food there, of which we want to get some. But the Badger, who has been digging towards it, always turns around, and we shall not get there. You come and scratch a hole for us and we shall give you a great deal of it." The Mole was at once willing and said: "Very well, I shall come," and went along with the Coyote. After entering the Coyote's house, the Mole at once commenced to dig a hole underground, which he did very rapidly. The Badger followed him, enlarging the hole. The Coyote followed the Badger and scratched out the loose dirt.

They arrived at a place not far from the rock where the food had been placed the day before. Here the Mole made a small opening and looked out and saw that the people were just arriving, and that the maidens again placed the food near the rock. So, the Mole continued his digging to the place where the food was, and while the Hopi were at work, he reached all the food to his companions. The Mole handed it to the Badger, the Badger to the Coyote, and the latter carried it to his house. When the Hopi were through with their work the chief again said to the maidens that they should now go and get their food. They would eat and then go home. So, the maidens raced towards the rock where they had placed the food, but when they arrived here, they found all their food gone. They looked around and found a hole in the ground, but only for a short distance, because the Badger had tightly closed up the hole from the inside. "Well now," the maidens said, "somebody has put our food in here." So, the men and the youths brought their hoes and followed the opening in the ground, but they soon found that it was only open a short distance. Hereupon they abandoned it and went home hungry.

In the Coyote's house the three now divided up the food and the Badger and the Mole carried home their portions. On this they lived for some time afterwards. Soon afterwards the Coyote again visited the Badger. The Badger had cut up into small pieces some lolo'okongs and roasted them. They were very fat. This food he set before his friend, the Coyote, and with it some comiviki. The Coyote ate the food with relish. "But that tastes well," he said; "what is it? Where did you get it?" "Why, I opened my side," the Honani said. "My intestines are covered with much fat, and I took out some of that fat and prepared this food from it," "Did it not hurt you," the Coyote asked, "when you opened your body?" "No," the Badger replied, "I opened it, took out the fat, and you see there is nothing the matter with my body. With this knife here I opened my body," showing the knife to the Coyote. "Very well," the Coyote said, "I am going to take this knife along and I am going to do the same, so to-morrow you must visit me, too." Hereupon he left and went home.

The Badger laughed, saying: "That Fool Old Man (Una Wuhtaka) believes that I took that fat out of my body."

The next morning the Coyote took the knife and commenced to cut into his abdomen. It hurt him very much, 'and as he was cutting, he moaned, "Ana-na-na," but he kept on cutting and the blood was running out profusely.

When he had cut through the abdomen wall, he took hold of the fat and commenced to pull at it, but before he got through, he became exhausted and fell down and died. When his friend, the Badger, arrived he found the Coyote lying there dead. "That Fool Old Man," he said, "thinking that I extracted that fat from my body!" And thus, the Badger killed his friend, the Coyote.

When the World was Young
(Blackfoot)

When the world was young, Old Man and Old Woman Coyote were walking around. "Let us decide how things will be," Old Man Coyote Said.

"That would be good," said Old Woman Coyote. "How shall we do it?"

"It was my idea so I'll have the first say" said Old Man Coyote.

"That is fine," said Old Woman Coyote. "Just as long as I have the last say."

So, for a while they walked around looking at things. Finally Old Man Coyote said something. "The men will be the hunters. Any time they want to shoot an animal they will call it and it will come."

"I too think men should be the hunters," said Old Woman Coyote. "But if the animals come so easily then life will be too easy for the people. The animals shall run away and hide. This will make it harder for the hunters but it will make them smarter and stronger."

"You have the last say," said Old Man Coyote.

They walked around some more and again Old Man Coyote said something. "I've been thinking about how people will look. They will have eyes on one side of their face and their mouth on the other. Their mouths will go up and down. They will have ten fingers on each hand."

"I too think that people should have their eyes and their mouth on their faces, but their eyes will be at the top of their face and their mouth at the bottom and they will be across from each other." Said Old Woman Coyote "and I agree they should have fingers, but ten on each hand will be too awkward. They will have 5 fingers on each hand."

"You have the last say," said Old Man Coyote.

They continued to walk and finally they were by the river when Old Man Coyote spoke. "Let us decide about life and death. I will do it this way. I will throw this buffalo chip into the river. If it floats, then when people die, they will come back to life after 4 days and live forever."

Old Man Coyote threw the chip in and it floated.

"I too think we should decide this way," Old Woman Coyote said. "But we will use a stone instead of a buffalo chip. I will throw this stone in the river. If it floats then people will come back in 4 days and live forever. If it sinks then people will not come back to life after they die."

Old Woman Coyote threw the stone in the river and it sank.

"That is the way it should be," Old Woman Coyote said. "If people lived forever the Earth would get to crowded and there would not be enough food. This way people will learn compassion."

Old Man Coyote said nothing.

Some time passed. Old Woman Coyote had a child. She and Old Man Coyote loved the child a lot and they were happy.

One day, the child became ill and died. Then Old Woman Coyote went to Old Man Coyote.

"Let us have our say again about death," she said.

But Old Man Coyote shook his head." NO, you had the last say."

———

White Crow Hides the Animals

Out on the plains there was a camp where the hunters were never successful. They could not understand this. Every time they went out to hunt, the game scattered and hid where it could not be killed. This caused the people to starve.

The people did not know that there was someone who went out and told all the buffalo and deer within reach that the hunters were coming and to hide. There was a man in camp who could turn himself into a white crow. He went out and told all the animals to make their getaway. This person, White Crow, would come back later in the day when no one could see him and turn himself back into a man.

The starving people moved their camp in various directions trying to find where the game went. White Crow did not move. Under his lodge was a hole where all the buffalo were. This is where he got his food.

When the people returned to one camp, they found this man still living there. He said, "Why did you come back? I have nothing to eat. I have been having just as hard a time as you. I have had nothing to eat since you left."

One day, some of the men were playing a game with sticks and White Crow came toward them. The players smelled the odor of buffalo fat coming from the direction where the man was standing. They noticed that the man had on a good-looking buffalo hide, turned inside out to disguise its newness. He also had a sacred stick rubbed with buffalo fat that they could smell. He did not like their looking at him. He slipped away so they could not ask him questions.

Coyote was there in that village. That night he called the men together and offered to look around White Crow's camp and tell them what he learned. Coyote watched White Crow's camp for a while, the came back and told the men he needed two good men with good eyes. Owl and Dragonfly were the ones chosen. Coyote told them to lie down in the grass and watch White Crow wherever he went. Dragonfly watched so hard, his eyes came out. Owl strained his eyes until they became larger than ordinary eyes. Owl watched the man until he saw him go down in the ground.

When Owl came back, coyote told the men to gather everyone together and announce they were moving camp. Coyote was going to change himself into a little pup and they were to leave him behind. White Crow had a daughter, Coyote told them. "When the people leave, she will search the camp for anything left behind and will find me."

The next day, everyone moved and Coyote turned himself into a dog, but he forgot to put on the whiskers of a dog. The little girl found him and brought him to her lodge. When White Crow came in, he asked to examine the dog. He saw that there were no whiskers and he told his daughter that he was afraid of this. He said it was a person disguised as a dog. But the girl said she wanted to keep it anyway. She refused to throw it away. She gave it a piece of meat while her father went out to warn all the game to be alert.

One day when the man was gone, the little girl removed the stone that covered the buffalo hole. She called the puppy over to look into the hole but he acted as if her were afraid. "Come over here. Look in here pup, see what we have." When she said this, the pup came over. Suddenly he jumped into the hole, and turned into a man and began to holler, "Scatter all over the world! Scatter! Scatter!" The buffalo came out of the ground like a big river. Coyote turned himself into a cocklebur and stuck himself on the fetlock of the last buffalo that go past the girl, who was waiting for him with a club. After the buffalo got out of White Crow's lodge and were a long way off, Coyote became a man again and shouted "Scatter! Scatter!"

When White Crow returned to his camp and saw what had happened, he said to the young girl, "See what you have done! I was afraid something like this would happen. Now we are going to have a hard time."

Coyote returned to his people and they began to enjoy the buffalo again. This made White Crow angry. He directed the buffalo and the other animals to hide from the hunters. Soon the people were starving again. White Crow let them know he was going to make it harder than before. He flew over the camp saying, "I want you to know it was me who kept you from killing the buffalo before. You are not going to kill meat animals any more."

That night, Coyote called the men together and told them he had a plan. They would have to follow his instructions carefully. They were to announce that everyone should move over to a forest a few valleys away. Coyote would turn himself into a bull elk and hide in the brush where

White Crow would not see him. When the people came along, they were to kill and butcher him, but they were to leave behind his skeleton and his head with the antlers attached.

So, the next morning, the people moved to where he had directed them and some of them went out to look for game. A hunter scared up the elk, chased him, and killed him. They butchered him the way they had been told.

While they had been chasing him, White Crow had flown over Elk and said, "I wonder how I overlooked you. I should have told you they were hunting and to hide. I am to blame. But you can run fast and save yourself."

After the hunters left: White Crow found the skeleton. He sat on its antlers and thought to himself, "I know this is not an elk, I know what Coyote did before. This is just Coyote, who has disguised himself again. I will test him and find out." So White Crow stood on Elk's head and began to strike at Elk's nose with his sharp beak saying, "I know you are Coyote! I know you are Coyote!" He kept on striking. He stopped just as Coyote was about to cry out. "Well, I will try another place." He moved back to the hind leg, to the kneecap. He struck with his beak. "I know you are Coyote! I know you are Coyote!" Again, Coyote was just about to yell when White Crow stopped.

"Well, you must be an elk, but I do not see how I overlooked you." White Crow than decided he would pick out the scraps of meat left on the ribs. When he stuck his head in between them, Coyote closed his ribs and held White Crow in a vise. Then he got up and turned himself into a man. "Now, I have got you!"

White Crow said, "Coyote, please turn me loose. I will not do anything bad again. I will be good to you all. Please, turn me loose!"

The people were watching from a distance and when they saw that Coyote had White Crow, they began to shout.

Coyote said, "Now I have caught you and I am going to take you to camp and let the people do as they please with you." He took him to the camp and the people said, "This is the one who has caused us a lot of misery and starved us. Now that we have him, what shall we do with him?"

Spider Old Woman said, "Let me have him. I want to see the one who has caused us to starve." As she held White Crow, she was entangling him with her web but no one knew this. As she was doing it, White Crow got out of her hands and flew up into the air. He circled the camp, laughing. "This time I will have no compassion on you. This time I am really going to starve you!"

Coyote turned to Spider Old Woman and said, "I am going to tell the people to kill you for letting White Crow get away." Spider Old Woman said, "That White Crow doesn't know what he's talking about. I will get him." She began dragging in White Crow as though she was pulling on a rope. White Crow said. "Hey, I was only joking. I will be good. Have compassion on me." But Spider Old Woman went on pulling him in until she got him in her hands. She gave him to Coyote. "Do whatever you want with him," she said.

Coyote ordered the men to go and get firewood. They built a big fire and put White Crow in it until he was burned all black. Then Coyote said, "I am going to make it so you can never do anything your own way. All your life you are going to be a bird flying about looking for scraps. You are going to be frightened by everything."

Now, this is the way with Crow. (Kiowa)

The Girl Who Was the Ring

(Pawnee)
George Bird Grinnell, "The Girl Who Was the Ring."
Harper's Monthly, Feb. 1901

By the bank of a river stood a lodge, in which lived four brothers and their sister. The boys made arrows. To the branch of a tree in front of the lodge they had hung a rawhide strap, such as women use for carrying wood, to make a swing for the girl.

Whenever their meat was all gone and they began to get hungry, the girl used to send her brothers into the timber to cut dogwood shoots to make arrows. When the arrows were ready, she would get into the swing and the boys would swing her. As the swing moved, they would see dust rising all around the horizon, and would know that the Buffalo were coming.

Then all four boys would take their bows and arrows, and stand about the swing so as to protect the girl and not let the Buffalo come near her. When the Buffalo had come close, the boys would kill them in a circle all about the swing. They would quickly carry the girl into the lodge, and would kill so many Buffalo that the rest would be frightened and run away. So, they would have plenty to eat, and the dried meat would be piled high in the lodge.

One day the boys went out to get wood for arrows, and left the girl in the lodge alone. While they were away a Coyote came to the lodge and talked to the girl. He said to her: "Granddaughter, I am very poor, and I am very hungry. I have no meat in my lodge, and my children also are hungry. I told my relations that I was coming to ask you for food, and they have been laughing at me. They said, 'Your granddaughter will not give you anything to eat.' "

The girl answered him: "Grandfather, here is plenty of meat. This house is full of it. Take what you want. Take the fattest pieces. Take it to your children. Let them eat."

The Coyote began to cry. He said: "Yes, my relations laughed at me when I said I was going to visit you and ask you for something to eat. They said you would not give me anything. I do not want any dried meat -- I want some fresh meat to take to my children. Have pity on me, and let me put you in the swing, so as to bring the Buffalo. I do not want to swing you hard so as to bring the Buffalo in great herds. I want to swing you only a little so as to bring a few Buffalo. I have a quiver full of arrows to keep the Buffalo off."

The girl said: "No, grandfather, I cannot do this. My brothers are away. Without them we can do nothing."

Then the Coyote slapped his breast and said: "Look at me. Am I not a man and strong? I can run around you fast, after you are in the swing, and I can keep the Buffalo off. I can shoot clear through a Buffalo. I have plenty of arrows, and I need only use a single one for each Buffalo. Come on, I want to swing you just a little, so that but few Buffalo will come." So, he coaxed the girl, but still she refused.

After he had begged her for a long time, she agreed to let him swing her a little, and got in the swing. He began to swing her, at first gently, but all at once he pushed her very hard, and kept doing this until she swung high. She screamed and cried, and tried to get off the swing, but it was now too late.

All around -- from all sides -- the Buffalo were coming in great crowds. The Coyote had made ready his arrows, and was running around the girl, trying to kill the Buffalo and keep them off, but they crowded upon him -- so many that he could do nothing -- and at last he got frightened and ran into the lodge.

The Buffalo were now just all over the ground about the lodge, and suddenly one of the young Bulls, the leader of a big band, as he passed under the swing, threw up his head, and the girl disappeared, but the Coyote, peeping out of the lodge door, saw on the horn of this Bull a ring, and then he knew that this ring was the girl. Then the Bull ran away fast, and all the Buffalo ran after him.

When the Buffalo had gone, the Coyote came out of the lodge and saw that the girl was not there. He did not know what to do. He was frightened. Pretty soon he heard the girl's brothers coming. They had seen the dust, and knew that some one was swinging their sister, and that the Buffalo had come.

They hurried back, running fast, and when they reached the lodge, they found the Coyote just dragging himself out of a mud-hole. He crawled out crying, and pretended that the Buffalo had run over him and trampled him. His bow and arrows were in the mud. He told the brothers his story and said that he had tried hard to save the girl, but that he had not known that so many Buffalo would come. He said he had thought that the girl must be swung high, so that the Buffalo could see her from a long way off.

The brothers felt very sorry that their sister was lost. They counseled together to see what they should do, trying to decide what would be the best plan to get her back again. While they were talking about this, the Coyote, with all the mud upon him, stood before them and said: "Brothers, do not feel sorry because your sister is lost. I will get her back again. Live on just as you always do. Do not think about this. Do not let it trouble you. I will get her back again." After he had spoken thus, he said, "Now I am going to start off on the war-path," and he left them and went away.

He journeyed on alone considering what he should do, and at length, as he was traveling along over the prairie, he met a Badger, who said to him, "Brother, where are you going?"

The Coyote said: "I am going on the war-path against my enemies. Will you join my party?"

The Badger said, "Yes, I will join you." They went on. After they had gone a long way, they saw a Swift Hawk sitting on the limb of a tree by a ravine. He asked them where they were going, and they told him, and asked him if he would go with them.

He said he would go. After a time, they met a Kit Fox, and asked him to join them, and he did so. Then they met a Jack Rabbit, who said he would go with them. They went on, and at length they met a Blackbird, and asked him to join them. He said: "Let it be so. I will go."

Soon after they had all got together, they stopped and sat down, and the Coyote told them how the girl had been lost, and said that he intended to try to get her back. Then they talked, and the Coyote told them the plan that he --the leader --had made. The others listened, and said that they would do whatever he told them to. They were all glad to help to recover the girl.

Then they all stood up and made ready to start, and the Coyote said to the Blackbird, "Friend, you stay here until the time comes." So, the Blackbird remained there where they had been talking, and the others went on. After they had gone some distance farther, the Coyote told the Hawk to stop and wait there. He did so. The others went on a long way, and then the Coyote said to the Rabbit, "You stay here."

The others went on, and at the next stopping-place he left the Kit Fox; and at the next -- last of all -- he left the Badger. Then the Coyote went on alone and travelled a long way, and at length he came to the Buffalo camp. He went out to the place where the young Bulls used to play the stick game, and lay down there. It was early in the morning.

After a time, some of the young Bulls came out, and began to roll the ring and to throw their sticks at it. The Coyote now pretended to be very sick. His hair was all covered with mud, and his tongue hung out of his mouth, and he staggered about and fell down and then got up again, and seemed to feel badly. Sometimes he would get over near to where the ring was being rolled, and then the young Bulls would call out: "Here, hold on! Don't get in the way."

After a little while the Coyote pretended that he felt better, and he got up and went over to where the young Bulls were sitting, looking on at the game, and sat down with them, and watched the play with the others. Every now and then two of the young Bulls would begin to dispute over the game, each saying that his stick was the nearer to the ring, and sometimes they would wrangle for a long time.

Once, while they were doing this, the Coyote went up to them and said: "Here! You men need not quarrel about this. Let me look. I know all about this game. I can tell which stick is the nearer." The Bulls stopped talking and looked at him, and then said: "Yes, let him look. Let us hear what he says." Then the Coyote went up to the ring and looked, and said, pointing: "That stick is nearest. That man has won."

The Bulls looked at each other, and nodded their heads and said, "He knows. He is right." The next time they had a dispute, he decided it again, and all were satisfied.

At length two of the young Bulls had a very fierce dispute, and almost came to fighting over it. The Coyote came up and looked, and said: "This is very close. I must look carefully, but I cannot see well if you are all crowding around me in this way. I must have room. You would all better go over to that hill, and sit down there and wait for me to decide."

The Bulls all went over to the hill and sat down, and then the Coyote began to look. First, he would go to one stick and look carefully, and then he would go to the other and look. The sticks were about the same distance from the ring, and for a long time it seemed that he could not make up his mind which was the nearer. He went backward and forward, looking at the sticks, and stooping down and putting his hands on his knees and squinting, and at last, when once his face was close to the ground, he suddenly snatched up the ring in his mouth, and started, running as hard as he could for the place where he had left the Badger.

As soon as he had started, all the Bulls on the hill saw what he was doing -- that he was taking the ring away from them -- and they started after him. They did not want to lose the ring, for it was very useful to them, and they played with it all the time. When the Buffalo in the camp saw that the young Bulls had started, they all followed, so that soon all the Buffalo were rushing after the Coyote. He ran fast, and for a long time he kept ahead of the Buffalo, but they followed, a great mass of Buffalo crowding and pushing, running as hard as they could run.

At last, the Coyote was beginning to get tired, and was running more slowly, and the Buffalo were beginning to catch up to him, but he was getting near to where the Badger was. After a time, the Buffalo were getting nearer to the Coyote. He was very tired, and it seemed to him as if he could not run any farther. If he did not soon get to where he had left the Badger, the Buffalo would run over him and trample him to death, and get back the ring. At length, when they were close behind him, he ran over the top of a little hill, and down in the valley below saw the Badger sitting at the mouth of his hole. The Coyote raced down the hill as fast as he could, and when he got to the hole he gave the ring to the Badger, and just as the herd of Buffalo got to the place, they both dived down into the hole.

The Buffalo crowded about the Badger's hole, and began to paw the ground, to dig it up so as to get the Coyote and the ring, but the Badger had dug a hole a long way under the ground, and while the Buffalo were digging, he ran along through this hole and came out far off, and ran as hard as he could toward the brothers' lodge. Before he had gone very far, some of the Buffalo on the outside of the herd saw him, and called out to the others: "There he is! There he goes!"

Then all the Buffalo started again and ran after the Badger. When they had come pretty close to him, he would stop running and dig another hole, and while the Buffalo were crowding around the hole, trying to dig him out, he would dig along under the ground, until he had got far beyond them, and would then come to the top of the ground, and run as fast as he could toward the lodge. Then the Buffalo would see him and follow him.

In this way he went a long distance, but at length he got tired and felt that he could not run or dig much farther. He was almost spent. At last, when he dug out of the ground, he saw not far off the Kit Fox, lying curled upon a rock, asleep in the sun. He called out: "Oh, my brother, I am almost tired out! Help me! "

The Kit Fox jumped up and ran to him and took the ring in his mouth and started running, and the Badger dug a deep hole, and stayed there. The little Fox ran fast, gliding along like a bird; and the Buffalo, when they saw him running, chased him and ran hard. The Kit Fox is a swift animal, and for a long time he kept ahead of the Buffalo.

When he was almost tired out, he came to where the Rabbit was, and gave him the ring, and ran into a hole, and the Rabbit ran on. The Buffalo followed the Rabbit, but he ran fast and kept ahead of them for a long time. When they had almost caught him, he came to where the Hawk was sitting.

The Hawk took the ring in his claws and flew off with it, and the Rabbit ran off to one side and hid in the long grass. The Buffalo followed the Hawk, and ran after him. They seemed never to get tired. The Hawk, after he had been flying a long time, began to feel very weary. He would sail down low over the Buffalo's backs, and was only just able to keep above them. At last, he got near to where the

Blackbird was.

When the Blackbird heard the pounding of many hoofs and knew that the Buffalo were coming, he flew up on a sunflower stalk and waited. When the Buffalo came to the place where he was, he flew up over them to the Hawk, and took the ring on his neck, and flew along over the Buffalo. The ring was heavy for so small a bird, and he would alight on the backs of the Buffalo and fly from one to another. The Buffalo would toss their heads and try to hit him with their horns, but he kept flying from one to another, and the Buffalo behind were always pushing forward to get near the ring, and they pushed the other Buffalo ahead of them. Pretty soon the herd passed over a hill and were rushing down to the place on the river where the brothers' lodge stood.

Ever since their sister had been lost, the brothers had been making arrows, and now they had piles of them stacked up about the lodge. When they saw the Buffalo coming, they got their bows and took their arrows in their hands, and shot and shot until they had killed many, many Buffalo, and the rest were frightened and ran away.

The Blackbird had flown into the lodge with the ring, and after the brothers had finished killing, they went into the lodge. And there, sitting by the fire and smiling at them as they came in, they saw their sister.

Coyote and the Rattlesnake

(Sia of New Mexico)
Katharine Berry Judson,
Myths and Legends of
California and the Old
Southwest, 1912

Coyote's house was not far from Rattlesnake's home. One morning when they were out walking together, Coyote said to Rattlesnake, "To-morrow come to my house." In the morning Rattlesnake went to Coyote's house. He moved slowly along the floor, shaking his rattle. Coyote sat at one side, very much frightened. The movements of the snake and the rattle frightened him. Coyote had a pot of rabbit meat on the fire, which he placed in front of the snake, saying, "Companion, eat."

"I will not eat your meat. I do not understand your food," said Rattlesnake. "What food do you eat?" "I eat the yellow flowers of the corn." Coyote at once began to search for the yellow corn flowers. When he found some,

Rattlesnake said, "Put some on top of my head so that I may eat it." Coyote stood as far off as he could and placed the pollen on the snake's head. The snake said, "Come nearer and put enough on my head so that I may find it." Coyote was very much afraid, but after a while he came nearer and did as he was told. Then the snake went away, saying, "Companion, to-morrow you come to my house." "All right," said Coyote. To-morrow I will come." Coyote sat down and thought about the morrow. He thought a good deal about what the snake might do. So, he made a small rattle by placing tiny pebbles in a gourd and fastened it to the end of his tail. He shook it a while and was much pleased with it. The next morning, he started for the snake's house. He shook the rattle on the end of his tail and smiled, and said to himself, "This is good. When I go into Rattlesnake's house, he will be very much afraid of me."

Coyote did not walk into Snake's house, but moved like a snake. But Coyote could not shake his rattle as the snake shook his. He had to hold it in his hand. But when he shook his rattle, the snake seemed much afraid, and said, "Companion, I am afraid of you."

Now Rattlesnake had a stew of rats on the fire, and he placed some before Coyote. But Coyote said, "I do not understand your food. I cannot eat it because I do not understand it."

Rattlesnake insisted upon his eating, but Coyote refused. He said, "If you put some of the flower of the corn on my head, I will eat. I understand that food." The snake took some corn pollen, but he pretended to be afraid of Coyote and stood off some distance. Coyote said, "Come nearer and place it on top my head."

Snake replied, "I am afraid of you." Coyote said, "Come nearer. I am not bad." Then the snake came closer and put the pollen on top of Coyote's head. But Coyote did not have the long tongue of the snake and he could not get the pollen off the top of his head. He put out his tongue first on one side of his nose and then on the other, but he could only reach to the side of his nose. His efforts made the snake laugh, but the snake put his hand over his mouth so Coyote should not see him laugh. Really, the snake hid his head in his body.

At last Coyote went home. As he left the snake's house, he held his tail in his hand and shook the rattle. Snake cried, "Oh, companion! I am so afraid of you!" but really the snake shook with laughter.

When Coyote reached his home, he said to himself, "I was such a fool. Rattlesnake had much food to eat and I would not take it. Now I am very hungry." Then he went out in search of food.

The Offended Rolling Stone

*(Pawnee)
Dorsey,
Publications of
the Carnegie
Institution, lix,
446, No. 126*

Coyote was going along, and as he had not had anything to eat for some time, he was very hungry. In the evening he went to a high hill and sat down. Early the next morning he started again. He came to a big round stone.

He took out his knife and said: "Grandfather, this knife I give to you as a present. I want you to help me to get something to eat."

Coyote went over a hill, and there in the bottom was a village of people. He went into the village and he could see meat hanging on poles everywhere in the camp. He went into one of the tipis and the people in the tipi roasted a piece of meat for him. just as he was about to taste of the meat he thought of his knife and said: "Why did I give my knife to that stone? I should have kept it and then I should have been able to cut the meat without having to pull it with my hands." He asked to be excused and went out.

He went to where the stone was. He said: "Grandfather, I will have to take back this knife, for I have found a village of people with plenty of meat." He went over the hills and into the bottom, but there was no village there. Coyote went back and returned the knife to the stone. He went back over the hills and there saw the village and he entered one of the tipis.

They placed before him some meat. He began to chew the meat. He thought of his knife. He went back to the stone, and as he took the knife the stone said: "Why do you take the knife away from me? I am now going to kill you."

Then the stone ran after the Coyote. Coyote ran and came to a den of Bears. He told the Bears that a person was running after him and he asked them to help him. The Bears said that they were not afraid of anything. They asked what the thing was, and he said it was the stone. The Bears said: "Keep on running.

We can not do anything with the stone." The stone was close to Coyote when he came up to another den of Mountain-Lions. They also told Coyote to pass on, as they could not do anything for him. After a while, Coyote came to a Buffalo standing all alone, but when the Buffalo found out that it was the stone running after Coyote, he told him to pass on.

At last Coyote came to a place where the Bull-Bats stayed. Coyote said: "Grandchildren, there is a person running after me." The Bull-Bats then said: "Enter our lodge and remain there." When the stone came rolling up it said: "Where is that person who came here?" The Bull-Bats did not reply and the stone became angry.

Then the Bull-Bats said: "He is here and we are going to protect him." The Bull-Bats flew up and then down, and they expelled flatus on the stone. Every time they did this a piece broke off from the stone. The largest Bull-Bat came down and expelled flatus right on the center and broke the stone into pieces. Then the Coyote was told to come out and go on his way.

Coyote started off, and when he got over the hills he turned around and yelled at the Bull-Bats and said: "All you big-nosed funny things, how you did behave to that stone." The Bull-Bats heard it and did not pay any attention, but he kept on making fun of them. Then the Bull-Bats flew up in a group, and came down, and with their wings they got the stones together again and started it to rolling, and said: "Go and kill that fellow."

The stone then ran after Coyote and Coyote tried to get away, but he could not. At last, he gave out. He jumped over a steep bank and the stone was right behind him. As Coyote struck the bottom, the stone fell on him and killed him. This is why we used to find dead coyotes in the hills and valleys.

Coyote's Eyes

(Pima from Arizona)
Katharine Berry Judson, Myths and Legends of California
and the Old Southwest, 1912

When Coyote was traveling about one day, he saw a small
bird. The bird was hopping about contentedly and Coyote
thought, "What a beautiful bird. It moves about so
gracefully."

He drew nearer to the bird and asked, "What beautiful
things are you working with?" but the bird could not
understand Coyote. After a while the bird took out his two
eyes and threw them straight up into the air, like two
stones. It looked upward but had no eyes. Then the bird
said,

"Come, my eyes. Come quickly, down into my head." The
eyes fell down into the bird's head, just where they
belonged, but were much brighter than before.

Coyote thought he could brighten his eyes. He asked the
bird to take out his eyes. The bird took out Coyote's eyes,
held them for a moment in his hands, and threw them
straight up into the air. Coyote looked up and called,

"Come back, my eyes. Come quickly."

They at once fell back into his head and were much brighter than before. Coyote wanted to try it again, but the bird did not wish to. But Coyote persisted.

Then the bird said, "Why should I work for you, Coyote? No, I will work no more for you." But Coyote still persisted, and the bird took out his eyes and threw them up.

Coyote cried, "Come, my eyes, come back to me."

But his eyes continued to rise into the air, and the bird began to go away. Coyote began to weep. But the bird was annoyed, and called back, "Go away now. I am tired of you. Go away and get other eyes."

But Coyote refused to go and entreated the bird to find eyes for him. At last, the bird gathered gum from a pinon tree and rolled it between his hands and put it in Coyote's eye holes, so that he could see.

But his eyes had been black and very bright. His new eyes were yellow.

"Now," said the bird, it "go away. You cannot stay here any longer."

Coyote Proves Himself a Cannibal

(Jicarilla Apache) Text Frank Russell, Myths of the Jicarilla Apaches, 1898

Owl was the one who had arrows. He had a club also with which he killed men whom he ate. "Up at the low gap I am watching for men, wuu hwuu woo," he sang. Coyote came walking along in front of him. "Wuu hwuu woo," sang Owl, "I am looking for men in the low gap." The two came face to face there.

"Now," said Owl, "the one who vomits human flesh will kill men."

"Very well," said Coyote, "shut your eyes." Owl shut his eyes. When he vomited, Coyote put his hand under and took the meat. The grasshoppers which Coyote vomited he put in Owl's hand. "Now open your eyes," said Coyote. Owl looked and saw the grasshoppers lying in his hand. Coyote showed him the meat. "What did I tell you?" said Coyote, "this is the meat I threw up." "Where did I drink in the grasshoppers?" said Owl.

Coyote ran all around Owl. "Because I run fast like this, I eat people," said Coyote. "These legs of yours are too large, I will fix them for you. Shut your eyes." Coyote cut Owl's leg, trimming away the meat. He broke his leg with a stone and took the arrows away leaving him only the club.

Coyote ran around Owl who threw his club at him. He

would say, "Come back, my club," and it would come back to him. He threw it again. "Come here, my club," he called. He hit him with it. Coyote said, "Wherever a stick falls when one throws it there it will lie." The club did not return to Owl.

"Now you will live right here in the canyon where many arrows will be in front of you. Somebody might kill you," Coyote told him. Owl hitched himself along into the canyon. "Arrows painted black may kill you," said Coyote. Coyote went around in front of him and shot him with his own (Owl's) arrows.

After that everybody was afraid of Coyote, who went around killing off the people.

Coyote Keeps His Name

One time, Great Spirit called all the Animal People together. They came from all over the earth to one camp and set up their lodges. Spirit Chief said there was going to be a change. There was going to be a new kind of people coming along.

He told all the Animal People they would now have to have names.

"Some of you have names now, some have no names. Tomorrow everyone will have a name. This name will be your name forever, for all your descendants. In the morning you must come to my lodge and choose your name. The first one to come may choose any name he wants. The next person will take any other name. That is the way it will go. And to each person I will give some work to do."

All the Animal People wanted to have powerful names and be well known. They wanted to be the first to Old Man's lodge in the morning. Coyote walked around saying he would be the first. He did not like his name. He was called Trickster and Imitator. Everybody said those names fitted him, but he wanted a new name.

"I will take one of the three powerful names," said Coyote. "The Mountain Person, Grizzly Bear, who rules all the four leggeds, or Eagle, who rules the birds, or Good Swimmer, the Salmon, the chief of the Fish People. These are the best names. I will take one of these names."

Fox, who was Coyote's brother, said, "Maybe you will have to keep the name you have, which is Sinkalip. People don't like that name. No one wants it."

"I am tired of that name, Sinkalip!" said Coyote. "Let some old person who cannot do anything take it. I am a warrior! Tomorrow when I am called Grizzly Bear or Eagle or Salmon you will not talk like this. You will beg to have my new name, brother."

"You had better go home and get some sleep, Sinkalip," said For, "or you will not wake up in time to get any name."

But Coyote didn't go home. He went around asking the Animal People questions. When he heard the answers he would say, "Oh, I knew that before. I did not have to ask." This is the way he was. He lost his shirt in a game of hoop and stick, then he went home and talked with his wife. She would be called Mole, the Mound Digger, after the naming day.

"Bring in plenty of wood now. I must stay awake all night. Tomorrow I must get my new name. I will be Grizzly Bear. I will be a great warrior and a chief."

Coyote sat watching the fire. Mole went to bed with the children. Half the night passed. Coyote got sleepy. His eyes grew heavy and started to close, so he took two small sticks and wedged them between his eyelids to hold his eyes open. "Now I can stay awake," he thought, but before long he was asleep with his eyes wide open.

The sun was high in the sky when Coyote woke up. Mole made a noise that woke Coyote. Shed did not wake him up before this because she was afraid if he got a great name he would go away and leave her. So, she didn't say anything.

Coyote went right over to the lodge of Old Man. He saw no one around and thought he was the first. He went right in and said, "I am going to be Grizzly Bear. That shall be my name." He was talking very loudly.

"The name Grizzly Bear was taken at dawn," said the Great Spirit.

"Then my name shall be Eagle."

"Eagle flew away at sunrise."

"Well, I shall be called Salmon then," said Coyote in a quiet voice.

"The name Salmon has also been taken," said the Great Spirit. "All the names have been taken except yours. No one wanted to steal your name."

Coyote looked very sad. He sat down by the fire and was very quiet. The Great Spirit was touched.

"Imitator," he said, "you must keep your name. It is a good name for you. I wanted you to have that name and so I made you sleep late. I wanted you to be the last one here. I have important work for you to do. The New People are coming, you will be their chief.

"There are many bad creatures on the earth. You will have to kill them. Otherwise, they will eat the New People. When you do this, the New People will honor you. They will say you are a great chief. Even the ones who come after them will remember what you have done, and they will honor you for killing the People-devouring monsters and for teaching the New People all the ways of living.

"The New People will not know anything when they come, not how to dress, how to sing, how to shoot an arrow. You will show them how to do all these things. And put the buffalo out for them and show them how to catch salmon.

"But you will do foolish things too, and for this the New People will laugh at you. You cannot help it. This will be your way.

"To make your work easier, I will give you a special power. You will be able to change yourself into anything. You will be able to talk to anything and hear anything talk except the water.

"If you die, you will come back to life. This will be your way. Changing Person, do you work well!"

Coyote was glad. He went right out and began his work. This is the way it was with him. He went out to make things right. (Okanagon)

How Coyote Stole Fire
(Karok?)

Long ago, when man was newly come into the world, there were days when he was the happiest creature of all. Those were the days when spring brushed across the willow tails, or when his children ripened with the blueberries in the sun of summer, or when the goldenrod bloomed in the autumn haze.

But always the mists of autumn evenings grew more chill, and the sun's strokes grew shorter. Then man saw winter moving near, and he became fearful and unhappy. He was afraid for his children, and for the grandfathers and grandmothers who carried in their heads the sacred tales of the tribe. Many of these, young and old, would die in the long, ice-bitter months of winter.

Coyote, like the rest of the People, had no need for fire. So, he seldom concerned himself with it, until one spring day when he was passing a human village. There the women were singing a song of mourning for the babies and the old ones who had died in the winter. Their voices moaned like the west wind through a buffalo skull, prickling the hairs on Coyote's neck.

"Feel how the sun is now warm on our backs," one of the men was saying. "Feel how it warms the earth and makes these stones hot to the touch. If only we could have had a small piece of the sun in our teepees during the winter."

Coyote, overhearing this, felt sorry for the men and women. He also felt that there was something he could do to help them. He knew of a faraway mountain-top where the three Fire Beings lived. These Beings kept fire to themselves, guarding it carefully for fear that man might somehow acquire it and become as strong as they. Coyote saw that he could do a good turn for man at the expense of these selfish Fire Beings.

So, Coyote went to the mountain of the Fire Beings and crept to its top. He watched the way that the Beings guarded their fire. As he approached, the Beings leaped to their feet and gazed searchingly round their camp. Their eyes glinted like bloodstones, and their hands were clawed like the talons of the great black vulture.

"What's that? What's that I hear?" hissed one of the Beings.

"A thief, skulking in the bushes!" screeched another.

The third looked more closely, and saw Coyote.   But he had gone to the mountain-top on all fours, so the Being thought she saw only an ordinary coyote slinking among the trees.

"It is no one, it is nothing!" she cried, and the other two looked where she pointed and also saw only a grey coyote. They sat down again by their fire and paid Coyote no more attention.

So he watched all day and night as the Fire Beings guarded their fire. He saw how they fed it pine cones and dry branches from the sycamore trees. He saw how they stamped furiously on runaway rivulets of flame that sometimes nibbled outwards on edges of dry grass. He saw also how, at night, the Beings took turns to sit by the fire.

Two would sleep while one was on guard; and at certain times the Being by the fire would get up and go into their teepee, and another would come out to sit by the fire.

Coyote saw that the Beings were always jealously watchful of their fire except during one part of the day. That was in the earliest morning, when the first winds of dawn arose on the mountains. Then the Being by the fire would hurry, shivering, into the teepee calling, "Sister, sister, go out and watch the fire." But the next Being would always be slow to go out for her turn, her head spinning with sleep and the thin dreams of dawn.

Coyote, seeing all this, went down the mountain and spoke to his friends among the People. He told them of hairless man, fearing the cold and death of winter. And he told them of the Fire Beings, and the warmth and brightness of the flame. They all agreed that man should have fire, and they all promised to help Coyote's undertaking.

Then Coyote sped again to the mountain top. Again, the Fire Beings leaped up when he came close, and one cried out, "What's that? A thief, a thief!"

But again the others looked closely, and saw only a grey coyote hunting among the bushes. So, they sat down again and paid him no more attention.

Coyote waited through the day, and watched as night fell and two of the Beings went off to the teepee to sleep. He watched as they changed over at certain times all the night long, until at last the dawn winds rose.

Then the Being on guard called, "Sister, sister, get up and watch the fire."

And the Being whose turn it was climbed slow and sleepy from her bed, saying, "Yes, yes, I am coming. Do not shout so."

But before she could come out of the teepee, Coyote lunged from the bushes, snatched up a glowing portion of fire, and sprang away down the mountainside.

Screaming, the Fire Beings flew after him. Swift as Coyote ran, they caught up with him, and one of them reached out a clutching hand. Her fingers touched only the tip of the tail, but the touch was enough to turn the hairs white, and coyote tail tips are white still. Coyote shouted, and flung the fire away from him. But the others of the People had gathered at the mountain's foot. Squirrel saw the fire falling, and caught it, putting it on her back and fleeing away through the treetops. The fire scorched her back so painfully that her tail curled up and back, as squirrels' tails still do today.

The Fire Beings then pursued Squirrel, who threw the fire to Chipmunk. Chattering with fear, Chipmunk stood still as if rooted until the Beings were almost upon her. Then, as she turned to run, one Being clawed at her, tearing down the length of her back and leaving three stripes that are to be seen on chipmunks' backs even today. Chipmunk threw the fire to Frog, and the Beings turned towards him. One of the Beings grasped his tail, but Frog gave a mighty leap and tore himself free, leaving his tail behind in the Being's hand, which is why frogs have had no tails ever since.

As the Beings came after him again, Frog flung the fire on to Wood. And Wood swallowed it.

The Fire Beings gathered round, but they did not know how to get the fire out of Wood. They promised it gifts, sang to it and shouted at it. They twisted it and struck it and tore it with their knives. But Wood did not give up the fire. In the end, defeated, the Beings went back to their mountaintop and left the People alone.

But Coyote knew how to get fire out of Wood. And he went to the village of men and showed them how. He showed them the trick of rubbing two dry sticks together, and the trick of spinning a sharpened stick in a hole made in another piece of wood. So, man was from then on warm and safe through the killing cold of winter.

About the Author

Thanks for choosing this book, if you enjoyed it, please leave positive feedback.

G.W. Mullins is an Author, Photographer, and Entrepreneur of Native American / Cherokee descent. He has been a published author for over 10 years. His writing has focused on the paranormal and Native American studies.

Mullins has released several books on the history/stories/fables of the Native American Indians. Among his books are the extremely successful "Star People, Sky Gods and Other Tales of the Native American Indians," "Story Teller An Anthology Of Folklore From The Native American Indians," "The Native American Story Book - Stories Of The American Indians For Children Volumes 1-5," "The Native American Cookbook," and "Walking With Spirits Native American Myths, Legends, And Folklore Volumes 1 Thru 6."

He has released the complete series of his Sci/fi Fantasy books "From The Dead Of Night," including the Best-Selling titles - Daniel Is Waiting, and Daniel Returns.

His most recent work includes the series Rise Of The Snow Queen featuring Book One The Polar Bear King and Book Two War Of The Witches. Mullins' latest releases include two young adult fantasy series, Rise of the Darklighter Book One Dark Awakening and

Dream Walker Book One Enter the Sandman. Among his other releases are Messages from The Other Side (a nonfiction book about communication with the dead), and the soon to be released "Convergence" (a post-apocalyptic book multi-series event coming in winter 2021).

For further information, on the writing, visit G.W. Mullins' web site at http://gwmullins.wix.com/books.

Coyote Tales Of The Native American Indians

<u>Also Available From G.W. Mullins</u>

Daniel Awakens A Ghost Story Begins– From The Dead Of
Night Prequel

Daniel Is Waiting A Ghost Story – From The Dead Of Night
Book One

Daniel Returns A Ghost Story - From The Dead Of Night Book
Two

Daniel's Fate – A Ghost Story Ends From The Dead Of Night
Book Four

Rise Of The Snow Queen Book One The Polar Bear King

Messages From The Other Side Stories of the Dead, Their
Communication, and Unfinished Business

Vengeance

Mysteries Of The Unseen World – Ghost, Hauntings and The
Unexplained

Haunted America Stories Of Ghost, Hauntings And The
Unexplained

Timeless – A Paranormal Romance Murder Mystery

Star People, Sky Gods, And Other Tales Of The Native
American Indians

Walking With Spirits Native American Myths, Legends, And
Folklore Volumes One Thru Six

The Native American Cookbook

Native American Cooking - An Indian Cookbook With Legends
And Folklore

The Native American Story Book - Stories Of The American Indians For Children Volumes One Thru Five

The Best Native American Stories For Children

Cherokee A Collection of American Indian Legends, Stories And Fables

Creation Myths - Tales Of The Native American Indians

Strange Tales Of The Native American Indians

Spirit Quest - Stories Of The Native American Indians

Animal Tales Of The Native American Indians

Medicine Man - Shamanism, Natural Healing, Remedies And Stories Of The Native American Indians

Native American Legends: Stories Of The Hopi Indians Volumes One and Two

Totem Animals Of The Native Americans

The Best Native American Myths, Legends And Folklore Volumes One Thru Three

Ghosts, Spirits And The Afterlife In Native American Indian Mythology And Folklore

War Song: Tales Of The Native American Indians

Origin Tales Of The Native American Indians

Animal Tales Of The Native American Indians Vol. 2

More Star People, Sky Gods, And Other Paranormal Tales Of The Native American Indians